Andrea! Thank yc
Thank Help
So All your Help
Hugs!
a Marie Fostino

Sometimes Love Hurts

Marie Fostino

First Edition

"Love is patient, love is kind. It does not envy, it does not boast, it is not proud. It does not dishonor others, it is not self-seeking, it is not easily angered, it keeps no record of wrongs. Love does not delight in evil but rejoices with the truth. It always protects, always trusts, always hopes, always perseveres." Corinthians 13:4-8

It's going to be another night alone, Crystal thought. She put some chicken pot pie on her plate, and sat in front of the computer to eat and check her email. Blake had not walked in the door, and it seemed to have become a habit that he did not even call or text her to say that he would be late.

Crystal tossed aside her long brown hair with a few blonde streaks before settling in her favorite chair. She tightly clutched the pillow she had made for Blake for their first wedding anniversary. Lately, it seems, she had been crying so much because she was afraid that the man she loved so very much seemed to have stopped loving her in return. Tear stains covered the carefully knitted Bible verse on one side of the pillow saying, "Whatever God has put together, let no man separate." -Mark 10:9. She and Blake had been married just over a year, and she thought their love had just began to blossom. Her mind raced. It was impossible to stop thinking if something bad had happened to him – Was he injured? In some sort of trouble? Alone... or even worse, *not. What could I have done to upset him so much that he no longer wanted to come home to me*, she thought. The words kept repeating over and over again in her head, taunting her, and filling her heart with guilt.

Blake towered over Crystal at six feet tall compared to her five foot one height. His dirty blond hair and green eyes had her hypnotized since the day she first laid her dark Italian roast eyes, *what he called them*, on him. He was very kind and unforgettably thoughtful. In fact, he always complimented her on her clothing, hair, and accessories every chance he could.

Anytime she was upset or in a bad mood, he would act like her favorite Auguste Clown just to cheer her up so he could see that sweet smile of hers. They seemed to not only get along well, but have a lot in common, too. Both were enthusiastic about hiking, bike riding, and gardening, or so it seemed. Blake's church attendance with

her was spotless, where she served as the Second Grade Sunday School Teacher. Afterward, they would lounge around the house reading magazines, or work together on her flower garden. Blake enjoyed cooking new recipes, and Crystal loved being his guinea pig. He was good for her in every way possible; which made it even more difficult to understand what had gone so terribly wrong. His absenteeism slowly increased her own frustration causing her terrible headaches. Excedrin seemed to be her only comfort these days.

Crystal first met Blake, a restaurant manager, at the 7-11 store where she worked. She looked forward to his presence every morning and could not get enough of his smile or the sound of his velvety voice. Each morning when he would come in for coffee, he would always politely thank her for making it for him just the way he liked it. Finally one day he mustered every ounce of confidence he had to ask her out on a date. His hands were slightly shaking as he handed her a dollar bill to cover the cost of his coffee. There was not one person waiting in line behind him so he could take his time, but became frozen, moving at a glacial pace just staring at her. *How could she resist those beautiful green eyes peering into her soul like that?* Before he could even finish asking his question, she interrupted him with a humble yes. That is where their love story began, with politeness, simplicity, courage, and humility.

It was six pm on the night of their first date, and Crystal was anxiously waiting while looking out the window every couple of seconds. Any minute now Blake would arrive at her doorstep to take her out for dinner. She kept debating with herself if she should wait for him outside so she could just walk into the car when he pulls up, or inside and wait for the doorbell to ring before greeting him. She didn't want to appear anxious or desperate. She ran to the mirror to check on her hair and makeup one more time. There was this annoying cowlick that she inherited from her mother, and no matter the amount of Aqua Net Hairspray she used, it still made it's awkward appearance. While feeling defeated, she remembered a specific morning that Blake briskly walked in for his usual morning cup of coffee. He was running late for work and his shirt was buttoned incorrectly. She didn't have the heart to tell him; in fact, it was a side of him she had never seen, *an imperfect side.* A side that reminded her that he too was human, and it made him even more attractive to her. Her thoughts were instantly interrupted by the knocking on the front door. He had arrived.

She jumped at the sound of his knock and turned to run to the door. She slowed her pace, caught her breath, quickly ran her fingers through her hair, and stood for a few seconds behind the door with her hand on the doorknob. She could see his silhouette through the opaque window to the left of the front door. He hadn't left. He was standing there waiting for her. She casually opened the door and was pleasantly surprised by the bouquet of yellow daisies. That was her favorite flower! *How did he know?* She wondered. He must have remembered a conversation they had months ago. *How thoughtful,* she kept thinking as he followed her to the kitchen for a vase and water.

They seemed to hit it off right from the beginning. One of their favorite places to go was a karaoke bar where they ate burgers and took turns singing oldies.

She would never forget the night he asked her to marry him. They went to the karaoke bar, and to her surprise a bunch of her friends were there also. She usually saw a few of her friends, but it seemed like the bar was full of her friends. They ate, laughed, and watched as others got up to sing. They called Blake's name, and he winked at her before he took his place on the stage. When the music started she knew the tune, it was from Aerosmith, "I Don't Want to Miss a Thing". Blake had a fine voice, and she enjoyed watching him perform. As the song came to a close, he strode up to her and bent down on one knee pulling out a small, beautiful box. She drew a deep breath. *Was this really happening? Here? Now? In front of all these people?*

He said the words asking her to marry him, and told her he would be the luckiest man in the world if she accepted. Tears formed in her eyes as she opened up the box to peer at the delicate diamond ring nestled in satin. The bar was quiet, everyone waiting for her answer. She quickly wiped the tears that escaped and ran down her cheeks. She threw her arms around him crying yes over and over again. After their engagement, he sent her a text every day with some cute saying along with the closing line, *I love you always.* She was the happiest girl in the world.

"No wife of mine is going to work," he announced after their wedding. "I can support the two of us. Later when we have babies, your job will be to take care of them."

Taking his feelings into consideration, Crystal managed to keep herself busy by making their home a comfortable retreat. Blake often shopped with her on weekends helping to furnish their new home. They painted the house together, picked out the furniture together, and shaped the house they bought into their own individual home. Blake told Crystal she had a good eye for decorating. He seemed to appreciate the little things she bought, like lamps and knickknacks. Each piece had a personal meaning to them – the blue vase with the picture of daisies on it reminded her of the first time he gave her flowers, and the spot light she bought for the living room, reminded her of the lights in the karaoke bar where Blake proposed to her. Memories were wove into every corner of the house bringing her happiness.

Crystal's weekdays were full of cleaning and cooking, but in the evening around six pm Blake would come home holding flowers or a card with that beautiful smile she loved so much. He never went a night without telling her how beautiful she was, and how much he missed her. She loved the feel of his arms around her. It was always like magic – dinner on the table, followed by dishes together before retiring to watch television and lie in each other's arms. A night did not pass without fully giving themselves to each other, before peacefully falling asleep. Wedded bliss.

Over the past couple of months Blake had grown distant, and all of those beautiful memories seemed to sadden her. He just did not respond to her like he used to do. His restaurant was taken over by new owners, and he often arrived home late from work. What was more troubling is on the occasion when she would catch him sending a text before hiding his phone in his pant pocket. If she dared to ask him whom he was communicating with, he would grow angry and snap, "It's just problems at work."

She remembered when Blake brought her to his job to introduce her to his new bosses. "Hi, Katherine," said Blake after he introduced Crystal to the other new owners. "I would like you to meet my wife, Crystal." Crystal put out her hand to shake Katherine's, but Katherine barely touched Crystal's fingers with her handshake.

"Nice to meet you," Katherine said. "You know you have a hard working husband here, and I really appreciate him." Katherine shook her head to the side and smiled quickly before giving her head a jerk back. Her eyes landed on Crystal for a brief moment and then left.

"Thank you," she replied with a big smile. "I know he is a real gem."

"Well just to let you know, he will be quite busy for the next few weeks. Hope you will be alright home alone." It was silent for a few seconds. "Looks like you are busy yourself." She continued. "When is the baby due?"

"Soon," she beamed rubbing her belly. "We are both so excited." Crystal noticed that Katherine wasn't looking at her, but starring at her husband as they were talking.

"Right, honey?" She nudged, as she slipped her fingers around Blake's hand. He smiled and shook his head before giving her hand a squeeze.

"Oh, Blake," said Katherine. "Can I have a moment of your time in the kitchen?" She looked at Crystal. "You don't mind do you? He will be right back." Next she put her arm around his arm leading him to the kitchen leaving Crystal behind.

Ever since that day things had been different at home, and Crystal had doubts about the working relationship with her husband and Katherine. A woman knows, and Crystal could tell that this woman had a passion for her husband.

Crystal could not remember a specific time when it started, but somewhere along the way she began to feel lonely. After a couple of weeks dealing with her husband's strange behavior, she grew irritated and made sure to let him know it. After that, Blake did not even text her anymore to say he would be late. That's when she realized that something was horribly wrong. The days for her seemed so long and lonesome, and the nights were full of bitterness. When Blake did come home, he wasn't hungry, and went straight to bed. Although they still slept in the same bed, their backs were to each other. Neither one, it seemed, was willing or able to break the ice and speak first. Both were stubborn and blamed the other for this alienation of affection. As for Crystal, she had no idea how long she could bear this way of life.

Chapter Two
Broken Hearted
Present Day

As Crystal drove tears silently streamed down her face. All the while the sky was gray, and seemed to be crying along with her. With her endless tears and heavy rain slapping the windshield, it was all she could do to see the road in front of her. How she made it to her mother's house, she'll never know. The Christian channel blared on her car radio with the song, "Our God (Is Greater)". It always seemed to be during difficult times when she felt the need to bathe herself in Christian music. Between sobs she sang the chorus out loud, "*...then if our God is for us, then who can ever stop us, and if our God is with us, then what can stand against us...*"

Where are you now, God? She screamed in her mind.

Tires squealing, she turned into the driveway. She finally made it to the only place that made her feel secure. She needed to talk to her mother now, more than ever. First she texted Blake: **Gonna stay at my mom's for a while. Gonna give you some space and time with your girlfriend.**

Next, Crystal leapt from the car and raced toward her mother's comforting arms.

"There, there," her mother, Lisa, soothed, holding her tight. "Come in out of the cold, and tell me what's going on."

Crystal removed her jacket, showing off her new tummy before she turned toward her mother with eyes that were puffy and red. She had obviously been crying – a lot.

"Let me make you some tea," her mother suggested.

She gently put an arm around her daughter and helped her into the kitchen. You know what they say... *the kitchen is the heart of the home.* Lisa had just finished baking cookies, and the smell was inviting. Crystal grabbed a chair while her mother offered her a box of Kleenex before pouring the water into the teakettle.

"I just don't know what to do?" Crystal stammered before blowing her nose.

Lisa grabbed two coffee cups and placed them on the table.

"Take a deep breath, and start from the beginning, sweetie."

"Mom, we don't even talk to each other anymore," she stuttered between tears. "I don't understand why he doesn't realize that I need him, that *we* need him."

Lisa hustled around the kitchen as she listened to her daughter. The whistle sounded letting her know the water was ready. She placed tea bags in both cups, poured the water, and set some fresh baked cookies in the center of the table. Then, she grabbed a chair and nodded for her daughter to go on.

Crystal took a deep breath and let a few more tears fall before she continued. "I saw some lipstick on the collar of Blake's shirt today when I was sorting the laundry," she confessed. For a moment, she could not control herself as more tears gushed from her eyes. "What am I supposed to do with that?" She asked. "We're having a baby, and it sure looks like he's cheating on me!"

Although Crystal had been suspicious for several weeks, this was the first time she ever mentioned it to her mother, so it came as quite a shock. Lisa heaved a sigh before she spoke.

"Are you sure that he's cheating on you?" She asked ever so carefully. "It could be a hundred different things. Blake loves you. I see it in his eyes whenever he looks at you."

"Are you taking his side?" Crystal asked abruptly, her tone acidic. Her body stiffened and she stared at her mother like she had just lost her best friend.

"No, sweetie. I'm not taking any sides."

Crystal looked puzzled by that statement. All was quiet for a moment. They sipped their tea, and took bites of their cookies.

"Has dad ever cheated on you?" She asked breaking the silence.

Lisa shook her head no unable to sympathize with her grief stricken daughter. She thought back to the beginning of her marriage and how she was given a beautiful gift – her mother, *Crystal's grandmother's,* journals. *Maybe that was the reason she was meant to read those journals,* she mused. They had helped her to understand love to the fullest. She and her husband, Joey, had learned from her parents' mistakes, but perhaps for Crystal, they would prove to be the real test. She said a silent prayer, and asked God to provide her with the right words to say to her daughter.

"Honey, are you in a hurry to get home?" Lisa asked.

Crystal shook her head. She had not yet told her mom that she did not want to return home that night. She really needed to take a break from Blake.

"Good, let's take our tea and cookies into the living room. I want you to get comfortable as I tell you   a   story."

Curiously, Crystal followed her mother into the living room and settled on the couch. Lisa left and returned moments later with some journals in her hands that were tied shut with yellow ribbons.

"I'm going to share with you, my parents' past."

Crystal looked at her oddly. "Grandma and grandpa have been dead for years," she said. "I never even got to meet them."

Lisa took out their wedding picture and handed it to her daughter.

"These two people taught me more about love and life than I could ever teach you," she said, "and now I think maybe it's time they teach you about those things too."

"Beautiful picture, mom," Crystal said handing it back. "I see a little of you in her."

"Ha ha," Lisa laughed. "That's what my friends tell me when they see a picture of you."

Crystal smiled. It was a compliment to say that she resembled her mother.

"You need to call Blake to let him know where you are and not to worry about you. This is going to take a while, and you might want to spend the night if it's too late."

Crystal didn't mention to her mother that she already sent one. She leaned back on the couch ready to hear what her mother had to say.

"You know, honey, love and marriage are probably the hardest jobs you will ever undertake," Lisa began as she settled next to her. "I'm going to go back in time to a day when I was in college. That was over twenty-five years ago, but I remember it as if it were yesterday..."

Chapter Three
Ghosts of the Past
Lisa's Story

Lisa Da'mico lay on her parents' bed with her eyes closed imagining that her parents were still around her. She could still smell the Old Spice aftershave on her father's pillowcase. Her mind drifted back to a time when she was a child. Lisa rubbed vinegar on her father's head while he explained that his hair would grow if she massaged it. And she could still hear her mother laughing.

"You'd say anything to get a head rub from that child, wouldn't you?"

Her dad, Michael, extended his arm, squeezed Lisa's waist and whispered, "We'll show her, won't we? My bald spot will soon have hair again." Then he pointed out a few new sprouts of hair. Those made Lisa giggle and continue the hair rubs anticipating new growth.

That was such a long time ago. As Lisa lay on her parents' bed a few teardrops escaped from her eyes and ran toward her ears onto the pillow. She finished reading the journals her mother had made for her, and finally understood what her mother was trying to relate to her.

Lisa had been raised on the south side of Chicago. A college student, she attended Loyola University College. She was never one to worry much about her appearance. She had long brown hair that she usually tied into a braid and never wore much makeup – maybe some mascara on occasion, but she was far more interested in her studies than her looks. She planned to be a teacher, and wanted to be home with her children. That is whenever she eventually married and had them. Being a teacher would allow her to have each summer off, plus be able to spend holidays with her kids.

Sitting up, Lisa wiped her face dry with the back of her hand and thought of her dad again. His passing was still fresh in her mind. Michael had managed a bakery until he became ill. She wanted to remember the fun times she spent with him, like the day they all dressed up to celebrate Halloween with a party at his workplace. She and her parents all became clowns for the day. The bakery warehouse was decorated in a spooky manner with orange and black streamers falling from the ceiling, and matching balloons attached. They placed oversized cobwebs on the walls, and created a couple of large pretend spiders that appeared to be crawling toward them. They also played funny music like, "Monster Mash", and there were games, dunk for apples, and making mummies out of each other using toilet paper. To further the fun and the scares, a haunted house was created in one of the warehouse trucks. Some of the male employees dressed like zombies and vampires, and jumped out of the darkness to frighten all who were brave enough to enter. A couple of the men held power saws that hummed when they ran after some of the kids and their mothers. All that excitement made everyone hungry, so there were plenty of Sloppy Joeys, potato chips, and candy. It was perfect memory.

Lisa desperately needed to hang on to these memories because the last couple of years of her father's life were definitely not fun anymore. Michael's kidneys failed and her mother, Natalie, took care of him full-time. Lisa was living at school per her parents' request, while her mom was busy taking her dad to dialysis, trying to make him eat something each day, and constantly reminding him to take his medication. When he ran a fever, her mother rushed him to the hospital, and sat with him for hours on end. It certainly took a toll on her. She looked as though she had aged many years in just a short time. Finally when her father was too weak to climb the stairs to their bedroom, her mother had a hospital bed put into the living room.

It was one of the hardest things her mother ever had to do. Lisa remembered her mother telling her that after so many years, she dreaded the thought of him not being in the bedroom with her.

Night after night as he grew weaker and weaker, her mother often fell asleep on a recliner beside her father's new bed so she could be near him. Her father had lost a lot of weight. His face lacked depth, and his mental state deteriorated rapidly. When he made a sudden move or his breathing turned too shallow, her mother made sure she was nearby. Eventually, oxygen was delivered to the house to help him breathe. The apparatus included tubing with prongs that went into his nose called a nasal cannula. Finally, they had to consider all of their options, and cried together as they talked about Michael possibly going into hospice care. But her mother chose to remain by his side. Some days she took out their photo albums and showed him pictures of their happy life together. Sometimes she put on one of their favorite old movies, and they watched it together. Still other times, she played music, stroked his hair, and simply held him hoping he would stay with her for just one more day.

The fateful day finally arrived and her father passed away. The funeral was held on a stormy day, which seemed appropriate as tears streamed from the faces of Natalie and Lisa as they stood at the burial ground. Lisa held onto her mother's waist while the wind slapped mercilessly against them. As they made their way back to the car, it was hard for either of them to believe that he was really gone. He had been a good husband and father. Both knew they would miss him dearly.

Lisa had never experienced death before and felt such a strong and painful tugging at her heart. Her mother whispered under her breath that she did not know how she could possibly carry on without him. Natalie's face was pale and her eyes puffy from all the tears she shed those last few days. She had always been a strong woman – the rock of the family. When she dropped her mother at home, Lisa did not think twice about promising to visit in a couple of days to check up on her. Natalie gave her daughter a kiss to show her appreciation and Lisa thanked God that she still had her mother. All of her energy would then go toward her.

Lisa was not sure she was ready to face her peers at college yet. However, she also knew it would be better to stay busy. She wanted her mind preoccupied with her studies so that she would not have too much time to think about the loss of her father. She filled her days with school, homework, and of course little thoughts of her dad creeping in from time to time.

It was the end of the following week before Lisa made her way back home. She knocked on the door and when no one answered, she slowly opened it and crept in. She found her mother sitting in the recliner in the darkness of the family room. The shades were drawn with the only light emanating from a tiny nightlight. Lisa silently drew close to her mother who was crying quietly. She knelt by her mother's side, and gently placed her hand on her lap – her heart breaking for her.

"Are you all right, mom?" She whispered.

"Yes, dear," she mumbled attempting to wipe tears from her face before she looked up.

A small smile crept onto her mother's face as she opened her arms inviting Lisa to come nearer. Lisa accepted and hugged her mother's neck. She could feel her frail body begin to shake as she tried to control her tears.

"You miss daddy, don't you?" Lisa blurted out without   thinking.

She did not mean to say what she had actually been thinking, but try as she might, she could not keep the wonderful memories of her father from filling her mind. She could not even study without hearing his voice reminding her how important it was to get a good education, or hearing him tell her how much he loved his little girl.

"Yes, I do," her mother whimpered.

"You found your knight in shining armor when you met dad, didn't you?" Lisa asked.

Her mother's frail smile seemed to widen with that remark.

"Yes," she replied.

"I mean you really found love. The kind that lasts forever, the kind everyone wants, but so many couples never   find."

Most of Lisa's friends parents were divorced. Many remarried and had blended families. Her friends often told her that she was in the minority, because she had the same mother and father throughout her life. That was something for which Lisa was very proud. Her parents had discovered the secret of staying married and being happy, and she wanted the same thing one day.

Her mother straightened up in her chair, and her temples creased. As she smiled, some wrinkles appeared.

"What does love mean to you?" She asked.

"You know," Lisa began, "the man you love and marry would cherish you, and only you forever. He would never hurt you, hit you, lie to you, or cheat on you. He would always want you by his side no matter what."

Lisa was still on her knees by her mother's side as her mom took her hand and caressed her head. She let her fingers comb through her long hair following it down to her shoulders.

"I want the fairytale, mom. Like Cinderella and Snow White." She glanced at her mother and smiled. "Like you had."

"Love is difficult, sweetie," her mom replied. "It's a choice, and it's not always that special feeling or the need for security. Oh yeah, it starts out that way, but then life goes on and sometimes it does hurt."

Lisa glanced up at her mother strangely.

"Have you heard the old sayings that love means never having to say you're sorry?"

Lisa shook her head. She hadn't heard that one before.

"Well that's wrong. You do have to say you're sorry. You must learn to compromise, and to forgive and forget. Love takes understanding, a ton of courage, and the unrelenting desire to stay together even when you feel totally betrayed."

Suddenly Lisa's head began to reel, and she could barely catch her breath.

What is she trying to tell me? She wondered.

She could not recall ever seeing her parents fight. Sure they had arguments and talked behind the closed door of their bedroom... *Wasn't that a natural thing to do?* She had so many questions, but decided it was not the right time to ask them.

"How do you remember your dad?" Her mother asked softly.

Lisa's memories of him were only happy ones. He went to work, they had dinners together as a family, and they went to church and on vacations together.

"I remember when dad was the coach to my softball team, and he helped me become the pitcher," said Lisa. Her mother smiled and nodded.

"I remember camping with dad. He tried to show me how to put up the tent, but then it fell on the both of us." Both girls chuckled.

When she was a cheerleader, her father came to the games to watch her. She was in her last year of high school when he became ill. At the time, Natalie noted how important it was that her daughter went on with her life as usual. She sometimes brought her dad to the games in a wheelchair so he could continue to be proud of his child, and also to give him as normal a life as possible. When Lisa graduated high school and summer came to an end, Natalie insisted that she move to the dorm so she could truly experience college life. She told Lisa not to worry about them, but rather to live her life and make them proud.

"I want you to keep those wonderful adventures stored in your heart," her mother said. Her hand began to shake and she removed it from Lisa's head as she began to weep.

"I miss your dad so much," she moaned. "I loved him with my whole heart, and I don't think anyone can understand how much it hurts that he's no longer around."

She grabbed a Kleenex and dabbed her swollen eyes.

"We had something so special between us. I don't know the words to describe our love." Then out of nowhere she sternly added, "Love and marriage is a full-time job. The hardest job you will ever have in your life."

Those words stuck in Lisa's head as they continued to talk throughout the night. Lisa spoke of the great times she had while growing up, and recalled some of the adventures they went on as a family. When it was time for her to leave, her mother was still in the recliner and ready to fall asleep. She said she could not bring herself to go back into the bedroom, that she had spent the last few weeks with her father in the family room, and that, *that* was where she could feel his presence.

Before leaving, Lisa promised to come back in a couple of days. However, she became so busy with homework from her professors that she did not return for a week. She found the house darkened and her mother motionless in the recliner where she had left her days ago. She looked as if she had not eaten or taken a shower since the last time she saw her. Her mother's face was drawn and pale. As Lisa tiptoed into the room, she noticed that her mother's eyes were closed. She gently brushed her cheek with her fingers. Her mother took a deep breath before opening them, and a faint smile crept across her face as she peered up at her beautiful daughter.

"Hi," her mother whispered.

"Mom," Lisa said in desperation, "can we go out tonight? Maybe to a restaurant and a movie?" All she could think of was doing something that would cheer her mother up. Lisa had never seen her like that before. Quite frankly, it frightened her.

Her mother reached out and touched her arm. "No, honey, but we can visit here. I don't feel like going out."

Lisa shook her head and tried to think of something else that might help her mother.

"Have you eaten yet today?" She asked making her way to the kitchen. She took out a pot to heat up some soup.

"No," her mother replied in a tiny voice.

In minutes, Lisa returned to her mother with a tray containing a bowl of soup and half a ham sandwich. They shared polite conversation as her mother insisted on hearing about her days at school. They then talked more about her father and how much they both missed him. Her mother's eyes twinkled whenever she said his name out loud. Finally, their tongues ran dry and her mother seemed tired, so Lisa decided it was time to go. While she put the dishes away, she noticed that her mother had eaten very little of her soup, and had only taken a couple bites of her sandwich.

"Will you be all right alone?" She asked more afraid than ever for her mother's welfare. "I can stay here with you, mom. It would be no trouble to go back and forth to school from here."

"No thank you, honey," she said faintly. "I do appreciate your concern, but I will be fine. You have a life. I had mine and now it's your turn, so go and enjoy it." She shook her head and added, "Honestly, it's okay. Go on now, I'll see you again soon."

Lisa hesitated before planting a soft peck on her mother's head with the promise to return in a couple of days.

The week went by swiftly with papers due for professors, and reading to be completed. By Friday, Lisa made her way back home. This time she found her mother lying on the couch lifeless with a photo album on her chest, and one on the floor. Lisa touched her hand but this time it was stone cold.

"Mom!" She screamed but her mother did not move.

Lisa's entire body began to shake uncontrollably. Her mother had always been there for her, but she had not been there for her mother. Although her mother had told her that sometimes bad things happen to good people, feelings of guilt and shame immediately consumed her being. She should have been there despite her mother's protests, and had only herself to blame. *How could she lose both of her parents in such a short period of time?*

Lisa later learned that her mother had lost the will to live since her father died, and she just wanted to be with him again. She died of a broken heart.

Chapter Four
Understanding Death
Lisa's Story Continues

The funeral came and went leaving the kitchen full of uneaten food. *Why do people bring over so much at times like this?* Lisa wondered.

With her mother's passing, the house belonged to Lisa or so her lawyer told her. It was written in the will, he said. The neighbors had opened the shades giving the rooms a peaceful look rather than the morbid darkness that her mother had kept it in during her last days.

Unfortunately, the glaring light revealed layers of dust. Her mother was unable to keep up the house for some time, which was quite unusual for her. In her better days, she was always scurrying around cleaning everything in sight.

As everyone left, they offered their condolences and reminded Lisa that if she needed anything at all, they were more than willing to help her. Only sweet things were said about her parents as they took turns hugging and kissing her cheeks. Some tried to smile and hide their tears, while others sobbed openly as they talked. It was an exhausting time in Lisa's life. but it was finally quiet after the last person left the house.

Lisa strongly felt the urge to get away, so with tears streaming down her cheeks, she made her way back to her college dorm. Thankfully, her roommates proved most comforting. They had brought flowers into her room and hung a big poster on the wall over her bed that resembled a card with all of their signatures on it.

"Hey," said Joey Henderson, who stood waiting for her in the lobby.

She and Joey had been dating over the last couple of years. Lisa considered him to be her best friend, her love, and the man she wanted to marry some day. Joey was six feet tall, and always wore dark clothing including a black trench coat. His bright blue eyes and long wavy golden blond hair captivated her. He reminded her of a hippy of the sixties. He was a year older than Lisa, and was studying computer engineering.

"How's it going?" He asked.

"Hi," Lisa weakly mumbled.

He leaned in and gave her a big hug. She really needed to feel someone warm and loving at that moment. She really needed him.

"I'm so sorry about your parents," he continued. "I told you I could have been there with you. Why did you have to go alone?"

Joey's eyes searched her face.

"I know," she replied. "It was just something I had to do alone... understand?"

He looked at her quizzically, shrugged his shoulders, and smiled. Lisa first met Joey at school in her freshman year of college, and they hit it off right away. She saw the love her dad had for her mom and she was looking for the same thing. Maybe, just maybe, she had found that with Joey. He was kind and considerate, and always seemed to put her feelings ahead of his own.

Lisa recalled the last time she had dinner with her mom, dad, and Joey. He had driven her to their house with flowers for her mom, and a bottle of wine for dinner. He always was such a gentleman. They had fun at the table, talking and kidding around during the meal.   Her mother had cooked manicotti with meatballs - Joey's favorite. Her dad had not felt so well, but just having company seemed to bring him back to his normal self. While the women cleaned off the table, Joey and her father went into the living room. They seemed to be in deep conversation and talked softly. Lisa remembered that when she walked into the room they were shaking hands, and Joey sported the biggest smile. She felt good that he was getting along so well with her folks. When she asked them what they were talking about, they both smiled and just said life.

Lisa decided to live in the dorm for a while longer until she could clean out the house. It was a job she certainly did not look forward to doing. The school counselor told her to take as much time as she needed to get her affairs together since she had lost both parents in such a short time, so she returned to her room for a good night's sleep. She wanted to start fresh in the morning.

Upon awakening, Lisa made a cup of coffee and then drove to her parent's house. As she strolled through the front door, she took her time examining the house.

The wall by the bathroom still displayed the markings that showed her growth from one year old to sixteen.　On the living room walls, pictures of every year she went to school were framed.　In the china cabinet was an 11x14 picture of her parents wedding day along with the china that her mother received when she got married.　Natalie only took those out each year for Thanksgiving dinner.　Her dad's favorite coffee cup saying Best Dad – the one Lisa had given him for Christmas when she was twelve – still stood by the coffee pot.　Her mother's plants sat by the window, most with leaves turning brown because they needed water.

Plenty of dust had gathered on the ceiling fans, on the tops of the pictures, and television sets. She suddenly shivered and hugged herself.　More fond memories and feelings of childhood rolled in and surrounded her as she walked from room to room. Ghosts of her past birthdays and holidays appeared before her, giving her that homesick feeling and making herself ask again, *"Why me?　Why God?　Why did you take both my parents from me so soon?"*

Hiking up the stairs, Lisa entered her old bedroom to find that the wallpaper had not been changed.　The ceiling still displayed the glow-in-the-dark planets and stars.　Ribbons from winning cheerleader competitions still hung on the walls. On the chair in the corner was the afghan her mother had knitted for her. On her dresser was a picture of her high school graduation, and another showing her with her parents. She was overcome with a warm and fuzzy feeling.

When she found herself at her parents' bedroom door panic set in and she instantly froze. As her eyes scanned the room, she noticed that the bed was still made with the pink and white flowery bedspread. The matching curtains still hung tied at the sides to let in the sunlight. A bookshelf to the left of the bed was full of fuzzy little animals that her parents bought each other during the holidays. There was also a large fuzzy gorilla with a rose in his mouth, and a big heart in his hands saying *I Love You*, as well as Raggedy Ann and Raggedy Andy dolls joined at the hip. When they were turned on, Sonny and Cher sang "I Got You Babe".

The shelf to the right of the bed was full of memories in pictures of her parents, and places where they had traveled. In one of them, her dad was holding a big orange fish, and her mother held a smaller one. She recalled that it was the time they went deep-sea fishing for their tenth anniversary. Another photo showed them skiing, sort of which made Lisa smile. Her father was lying in the snow with his skis pointed up in the air because he had just fallen, and her mother had quickly captured the moment. It was a trip to celebrate his thirtieth birthday. Still another showed her parents with leis around their necks, and a cruise ship in the background – a memory of their trip to Hawaii.

Lisa's legs stiffened as she stepped into their bedroom, but she willed herself to enter. She walked into their private bathroom and then their big walk-in closet. Her father's pants and shirts hung on one side of the closet, and her mother's dresses hung on the other. Memories flooded her head as she scanned the familiar clothes and the shoes on the floor. Then, she spotted her prom dress which she wore in the twelfth grade.

On some of the top shelves, she found photo albums along with shoe boxes full of old letters and cards that her parents, had given each other during their many years of marriage. On another shelf was a long white box with black paper hanging out of it. She grabbed the step stool and climbed up to pick up the box. Planting it on the bed, she opened it and saw her mother's wedding dress. Lisa felt she knew that dress very well from the lace that circled around her neckline to the pearls that were sewn on the sleeves. She had seen the dress in the wedding picture mom kept in the china cabinet. At that time, her dad had a full head of brown wavy hair that fell down to his collar, and bangs that swept across his forehead showing off his big brown eyes. Her mother said he reminded her of the members from the singing group called The Beatles. Lisa only remembered him with a bald spot in the middle of the back of his head, and his receding hairline. Back then her mother had long brown hair that she pulled into a French twist showing off her brown eyes. Dad was only five-foot six inches, so he did not like mom to wear high heels. She was only five-foot-three without them and he wanted to appear much taller than her.

Lisa pulled the dress out of the box to take a closer look. Her mom had always said that she wanted her to wear her wedding dress when she got married. Being a few inches shorter meant she would have to have it shortened – that is, if she really wanted to wear it. Lisa dreamed often about getting married. As she held the dress up to her, she noticed some journals beneath. They were tied together with a yellow ribbon ever so neatly. She picked up the top journal, her fingers trembled as she opened it. On the first page, a note was affixed with her name on it.

Dear Lisa,

I don't know how to put into words what I have to tell you. I am sorry for what I am about to reveal. I was diagnosed with acute lymphoma a few years ago. I never even told your dad. He was so weak, and we had all we could do to keep up with his medical bills and his dialysis that I decided I would just allow myself to live till God told me it was time to go home. I put this journal together for you slowly, at times when your dad was at dialysis and I was home alone, to describe how happy your father and I were, and how much of a blessing you were to us. I knew the time would come, and he would be going to heaven and I would be going soon also.   I hope this will bring you some comfort. Remember that we will always be in your heart, and that we love you very much.

Love,

Mom

Lisa took a deep breath before she began to read the journal. It was like sneaking into the heart of her parent's private life together.

I was only eighteen years old when I met your father. It was in the early 70's, and I felt like a flower child even though I did not smoke grass or take drugs. I put flowers in my hair, wore hip hugger bell-bottom jeans and big hoop earrings, and gave the peace sign to everyone I met.

It was a warm and fragrant day in the fall with lots of petunias. The trees held a multitude of beautiful colors. I remember because I was walking to the bus station. I worked in downtown Chicago as a page at The Chicago Title and Trust building. As a matter of fact, when I went to work I actually had to wear a dress and high heels. It was quite a distance for me to walk and catch the bus. Then, I had to take the A-Train and another bus, plus walk a few more blocks to get to work, but I loved it. I love the City of Chicago. To me, that city was like another planet. Nothing could compare to its beauty and culture.

One day as I was walking to the bus, a 1965 green Mustang pulled over to the side of the street ,and a young man asked me if he could give me a lift. I ignored him at first and kept on walking. As I tried to move along a little faster, my ankle gave way on me, and I tripped and fell to the ground - not very gracefully I might add! You can imagine how dumbfounded I felt, but that person immediately came to my rescue. He had rich brown hair that fell to his collar, and big soft brown eyes. He was there in an instant with his hand grabbing my elbow to help me stand up.

"My name is Michael," he said.

"Natalie," I responded, feeling my cheeks turn pink. Since my ankle hurt, I awkwardly accepted a ride to the bus. I did think of him at work, and was so surprised to see him at the bus stop again when I left that day for home.

"How's it going?" He asked after I got off the bus. "No more falls I hope."

I felt myself blush again with embarrassment.

"You weren't around to save me, so I had to wait until I saw you again," I said playfully.

He smiled, and our eyes met with a hint of something that made me feel a certain kind of closeness with him. Odd, since I'd never seen him before in my life. Instinctively, he asked me if he could drive me home. I hesitated while I mulled the idea over. He certainly was good looking enough, but was that a good reason to accept a ride from a stranger?

"Sure," I said finally, taking a chance.

He was a gentleman, and took me straight home with the promise that I would go out with him on Friday night. I dressed in blue hip hugger bell-bottom jeans, and a tie-dyed shirt that hung just to the top of my jeans. When I raised my arms, my tummy showed. My hair was long and straight. I parted it in the middle, and let it fall naturally down my back. I used to like how Cher dressed, and mimicked her in any way that I could; even the way she wore her hair. Michael showed up in blue jeans as well, with a blue shirt neatly tucked in his pants. He behaved like a perfect gentleman, opening and closing the car door for me.

He drove to an old nickelodeon restaurant, and when we walked in, there were big mirrors on either side like the kind that you find at the circus that make you look either tall or fat. That was an amusing way to start a date, laughing at each other. The lighting was dim, and tables with bench seats lined the walls. As we sat at our table, the bench suddenly moved with one side going upward, which I have to admit frightened me. As it went down, we both laughed aloud. Another interesting feature was the toys that lined the ceiling. Every time someone threw a coin at them, they made noises, like a monkey that played the cymbals or drums.

The food was just alright, but the atmosphere was so much fun. Beatles music, and tunes from the Monkeys and Frankie Avalon played in the background. It was drowned out every time someone hit a toy overhead. The joint was pretty full with people laughing and throwing coins. I don't think I ever had so much fun and laughed so hard.

"So what do you think of this place?" Asked Michael. He gave me another coin to throw, and I hit the monkey just right making the cymbals play again.

"This place is so much fun," I giggled. "I have never heard of this place before. How did you ever find it?"

He just smiled at me with those brown eyes shining. "I am glad you are having so much fun."

Next, the song "It's a Hard Day's Night" from the Beatles came on, and I started to softly sing it. Michael became amused with me, and was making fun of me by singing with a funny voice. Thank heavens we got drowned out every time someone threw a coin up to the cute animals with the cymbals.

This place seemed to break the awkwardness of a first date. It broke the ice, and gave us something to talk about on our way home.

"You know I do really sing," Michael said as he drove.

"I could tell," I laughed. "Your voice was so... so... I really don't have the words to describe what I heard." I watched as his face lighted up into a smile.

"Really." He added. "What would you say if I told you I also play guitar."

I turned my head to try and get a good look at his face. I wasn't sure if he was teasing me, or if he was for real.

"Yeah, really, I do. . . Well, I mean I did," he corrected himself. "I use to be in a band while in high school, and play at all the dances."

"Oh," I said, "So how many groupies did you have?"

After the date when Michael brought me home, he walked me to my door. He took my hands in his, stared deeply into my eyes, and told me I had the prettiest blue eyes he had ever seen. Then he gently kissed my hand.

"Natalie," he asked, "may I see you again?"

I quietly said yes hoping he could hear me since my heart was beating so loud. Be still my heart!

The following night, he came over and we went for a ride in his car. The sounds of Santana emanated from the radio. Michael told me that he played bass guitar, and was in a group that auditioned once. He told me they did not make it because a group called Styx just got a contract, and they sounded too much alike. We stopped for burgers at McDonald's, and talked some more. I learned that Michael was a year and a half older than me. He had attended college too, but had difficulty concentrating on schoolwork. Since his parents would only pay for his college if he *acquired A's in his subjects, he decided to drop out and continued loading trucks from a dock.*

We drove downtown to the beach, where we took off our shoes and walked along the water's edge. We continued to talk, and listened to the seagulls crying overhead. I truly enjoyed that time with Michael. He was so easy to talk with, and we certainly did a lot of it. In fact, we seemed to really hit it off. And each time our eyes locked, I noticed that his were an incredibly gentle brown.

The following weekend my cousin was getting married. and I was standing in it. I asked Michael to come and be my date. He paused and winked before answering with an emphatic "yes!" He picked me up right on time, and looked so handsome in a suit and tie. He certainly cleaned up well! In fact, I had to catch my breath when I saw him. Michael teased me about the maroon dress that my cousin made me wear, and after the wedding we snuck out of the reception to sit at the bar sipping cokes and talking away from the noisy crowd.

"You ever going to get married?" He asked.

I admit I was thrown for a loop by that question, but played it cool. I told him, "I guess some day when the right man comes along."

The band in the bar came back on and played a slow song.

"Want to dance?" He asked as we finished our cokes.

"Dance? No one else is dancing at the moment, Michael."

"This is my favorite song, and I'd love to dance with you," he prodded. "Would you please dance with me, Natalie?"

I fidgeted in my chair, and felt my cheeks flush.

"Come on," Michael whispered against my cheek. "That's what people do at a wedding."

He took my hand and walked me to the dance floor. No one else had gotten up, and it seemed as if a hundred eyes turned our way before a few people joined us.

"Is this okay?" Michael checked, and I couldn't help smiling.

"You know, this is fun," I noted. "What's this song anyway? You said it was your favorite."

"I have no idea, Natalie," Michael replied unabashedly. *"I just wanted an excuse to hold you close."*

And that he did. I loved being in his arms, and felt dizzy when he spun me around with the music. I had to admit that it was great fun being with Michael. He just went with the flow, and did not need a logical reason for doing anything. By then, the damage was done. I was falling for that man. I could not believe it myself. Everything was happening so fast.

When he brought me home that night, he walked me to the front porch.

"I have a question for you," he whispered against the side of my ear.

Shivers raced up my arms to my shoulders. "Okay," I whispered back.

"How do you feel about us so far?"

I softly kissed him on the cheek. "Like that."

He smiled broadly and whispered, "Me too."

Then he leaned in and kissed me on the lips. From that night forward, we were together all the time. He picked me up in the evenings from the bus stop and every weekend we kept each other company. We watched his favorite movie, Star Trek, *and played checkers or chess. We had become inseparable.*

Lisa put the journal down, sighed, and drew in a deep breath. Her mind was at ease for the moment. What she had just read was exactly how she envisioned things might have been with her parents. She got up and put the wedding dress back into the black paper inside the box before returning it to the closet. It would be the last room she would clean out, because there were just too many memories, and she was not ready to part with even one of them – at least not yet.

Lisa spotted a clay ashtray she'd made in the fifth grade sitting on the dresser. She had to mold it like a small snake and curl it around until it looked like a bowl. Then, she glazed it and chose a blue color before it was placed in an oven. Mom had set a pair of gold earrings in it. Neither of her parents smoked, but her mother said it would be great for her jewelry.

Next to the bowl was her mother's Esteé Lauder Beautiful Perfume Spray. She shook the bottle before squirting a few drops onto her wrist. She always knew when her mother was going out, because that was the fragrance of choice for any special occasion. The thought made her frown as she recalled how long it had been since her mother had actually gone out and worn her perfume. Her jewelry box was sitting there too, and Lisa opened it up to find her mother's favorite opal necklace with matching ring and bracelet. She picked up the dainty silver chain. Her mother always told her that she wore it on her wedding day, and was saving it for her to wear on hers. The colors within the opal were simply magnificent. Carefully, she tucked it back inside.

"Why?" She whispered out loud. "Why didn't mom tell me before that she had cancer so I could take care of her?"

Maybe because I had been so busy with school she did not want to be a burden on me. Suddenly she felt ashamed. *I should have noticed that mom was losing weight before dad's death. I should have been around her more.*

Tears gathered and burned behind her eyes, and she blinked to try to stop them. It was not long before Lisa found herself crying uncontrollably, her body trembling and feeling as if she were living a horrible nightmare. When she finally regained her composure, she picked up the journal and began reading where she had left off.

By the time the holidays arrived, we were inseparable. Christmas Eve came with small snowflakes that floated to the ground like little glass snowballs. That evening, Michael accompanied me to the Baptist church with my parents. Then we drove to his house for dinner. He was raised Roman Catholic, and his mother believed in the Feast of the Seven Fishes, which was comprised of different seafood dishes. Their dinner included fish, bread, and noodles. The house was full of relatives both young and old, and Santa showed up bearing gifts for the little ones, as well as a gentle reminder that they needed to go to bed early so he could visit their house again later that night. The house was full of laugher and love. We ended the night by attending a midnight mass at their Catholic church, which was spoken in Latin, and was so beautiful.

January came and went with Michael and I still together all of the time. We talked every day on the phone, and he picked me up each day after I got off the bus. He was starting to feel like he belonged to me, and I to him. It was the first week in February when Michael called me early at work.

"Natalie, hi. Can I ask you out on a date for Valentine's Day?" He asked in a rushed tone.

"Of course you can!" I giggled with delight.

"This is a formal date, Natalie," he said more seriously. "We need to be dressed up."

To be honest, I wondered what he was up to. On the night in question, he showed up wearing a classy suit coat and tie. I had purchased a formal purple dress with a sequined flower in the front just under the bosom. On the way to Kon Tiki Ports Restaurant in downtown Chicago, he made a point of telling me how beautiful I looked. What woman doesn't like a compliment like that!

Michael was still a true gentleman opening the doors for me and pulling out my chair. He ordered cordon bleu with mash potatoes and sugar carrots. After our tummies were full we strolled down a quiet Chicago street to enjoying the beautiful sights of the night. There was nothing more beautiful than that city at night. He took my hand and swung it gently in rhythm with our strides.

"Thanks for such a wonderful dinner," I said.

"No, thank you for letting me enjoy your company," he replied.

His fingers intertwined with mine as we walked for a while in silence. However, I could not help noticing that Michael seemed fidgety, like he had something on his mind.

"Natalie?" He finally said breaking the silence. We had walked to the river and were looking out over the water.

"Yes."

"I love you so much," he began.

I stopped walking and stared straight at him.

"I treasure everything about you. I miss you when we're apart for just a couple of hours. Every day when I'm working, I can't wait to see you that night."

He paused for a moment and took a deep breath. Then he pulled a little box out of his pocket.

"Natalie, will you marry me?" He asked, opening the box to display a gorgeous diamond ring.

I pulled back and looked directly into the soft brown eyes of that special man. How had I been so lucky to find him – or maybe, he found me. Either way, I could not help myself. The smile on my face grew bigger reflecting the incredibly wonderful way I felt inside.

"I love you, Michael. And yes, I'll marry you!"

Lisa closed the journal again, only this time feeling a warm sensation rush through her body.

Reflecting on what she read and reliving her mother's words in the journal, as well as watching her parents as she grew up, she knew this is what love is supposed to be like.

She tried to picture her parents on the streets of Chicago when her dad proposed to her mom. She had seen their wedding picture a thousand times and laughed to herself at the way they wore their hair, but she was also taken by the love they shared for each other. It gave her hope that someday she would find love just like that.

Lisa made her way to the closet again and pulled out the purple dress – the same one her mother wore when she got engaged. Her mother had told her a million times to please have it shortened. Since it meant so much to her, she wanted her Lisa to share it too. Her mom said that the dress brought her good luck, and she wanted to share her good fortune with Lisa. She decided to try it on. It was too long and the bosom needed to be adjusted, but it was so pretty. She felt like a princess in it. Fixing the dress would definitely be on her 'to do' list. Carefully, she took it off and hung it back up in the closet.

Lisa often watched her parents – the way they looked at each other, and how gently they spoke to each other. She missed them so much and began to feel a little queasy. Sadness overcame her, as tears found their way down her cheeks again. Maybe it was hormones that kept her eyes leaking. Or perhaps it was just a normal reaction to everything abnormal that had happened to her. She went to her room, took the afghan off the chair, and wrapped herself in it. She then recalled the time when her mother was knitting it for her. Lisa had watched her anxiously asking if she could learn how to knit too. Naturally, her mother said of course, but Lisa became too busy and never did take the time to learn that art.

Remember what you have to do, she reminded herself. She was supposed to clean out the house and go through everything that she had inherited.

However, she just did not feel ready yet. As she lay on her parents' bed taking in the surroundings, the smells, and anything that made her feel close to them, she wished with all of her heart that they were still around.

Lisa opened the journal again. *I want to share our wedding day with you*, her mother had written.

It was a beautiful spring day in April, the day before Easter - April 13, 1974. The sun was shining, but it was barely sixty degrees. A few clouds floated across the sky with the threat of a shower in the air, which I was told brings good luck to the bride and groom. My bridesmaids wore yellow dotted Swiss dresses and each of them held a partially closed parasol trimmed with lace and flowers coming out. The men wore dark pants with white shirts, and yellow cummerbunds around their waists.

My mother helped put my hair up in a French twist while my grandmother, who had made my veil, placed it on my head. My mother-in-law gave me the opal necklace, and placed it around my neck. She said that Michael had bought it for her, and she that felt I should have it. So I had something old, something new, something borrowed, and my garter had a blue ribbon on it for something blue.

I felt like a princess when I walked down the aisle with my father toward Michael. The church was full of relatives from both sides of the family. I could see the tears in my father's eyes as he kissed my cheek and put my hand into Michael's. I knew that they were happy tears, and that my father only wanted the best for me.

Your father was incredibly handsome in his white tuxedo with his hair trimmed nicely for the occasion. His smile was more radiant than I had ever seen it before. As we stood at the altar, he leaned in toward me.

"Are you as happy as I am?" He whispered. "You look incredibly beautiful."

I felt myself blush and gazed into Michael's eyes. I knew this was so right.

"I have never been happier or more sure of anything in my life," I replied softly.

We surprised our parents by giving them roses in the middle of the service while a couple sang "I've Got

You Babe". As I listened and repeated the words given by Pastor Clem, my heart sang too.

"I Natalie, take you Michael to have and to hold from this day forward for better or for worse, for richer and for poorer, in sickness and in health, to love and to cherish from this day forward until death do us part."

As Michael repeated those words to me, I began to weep, and tears slipped down my cheeks. The preacher followed by reading the verse from 1ˢᵗ Corinthians: "Love is patient, love is kind. It does not envy. It does not boast. It is not proud. It does not dishonor others. It is not self-seeking. It is not easily angered, and it keeps no records of wrongs. Love does not delight in evil, but rejoices with the truth. It always protects, always trusts, always hopes and preserves."

I took each word and carved them into my heart. What God had put together, let no man take apart. That was us, and our love. When the pastor introduced us as husband and wife and told Michael he could kiss his bride, the kiss seemed like it lasted forever. I don't think I had ever been so happy in my life. In the church parlor there was soft music playing as everyone enjoyed little finger sandwiches, while Michael and I cut the cake. Outside the window the sun continued to shine even as splashes of water drops hit the screen. I knew that good luck had landed upon us. I was the luckiest girl in the world to be married to Michael. I loved him so much.

Lisa set down the journal for a moment. Her heart pounded with excitement as she pictured her parents in her mind. She remembered one of the last conversations she'd had with her mother about finding her knight in shining armor. A smile formed on her lips as a few tears escaped down her cheeks. It was a comforting feeling to know that her parents were as happy as she had always imagined.

Chapter Eight
The Honeymoon & After
Natalie's Journal

Dabbing a tissue to her cheeks, Lisa re-opened up the journal and continued reading.

Lisa, we had a wonderful honeymoon. We took your father's car with a trailer attached carrying a motorcycle on the back of it toward Colorado. What a feeling of freedom I felt when your father drove me around the Colorado mountains on his bike. I don't know if I can explain in words the beauty of that state. The mountains were so high with a veil of white clouds hovering over them and on the very top you could see snow outlining them. I bet that's just what heaven looks like.

We found a cute little cottage that had a kitchen, living room, and bedroom for our two-week honeymoon. It finally felt like we were really married. I loved the idea of not saying goodnight to him at the end of the evenings. I also loved it when he held me in bed and made love to me. One day, we drove the motorcycle through the Garden of the Gods, a place with unusual and steep rock formations with beautiful scenic views. Must be what heaven looks like. The rocks had names like Cathedral Spires, Steamboat Rock and Balanced Rock. The beauty is hard to describe, and you could only feel peace and God's presence all around you. I did cartwheels on the Royal Gorge Bridge. Imagine this long skinny bridge that just maybe two cars could cross and so high above the ground - one of the World's highest suspension bridges – that makes everything below look like toys.

We found a place where fish were well stocked, and I fished for the first time. It was exciting to throw my line into the water and to see the fish fight over the bait. It was also a relief to know that neither one of us had to clean them. We waited afterward to get them gutted, and then went back to our honeymoon cottage with an ice chest of freshly cleaned fish. We cooked, ate, and watched television just like a married couple – which we were! It was kind of funny because we really didn't know each other very well or for very long, but we knew we loved each other and wanted to make it work.

Before we knew it, the two weeks had flown by. Of course all good things must come to an end, and we had to return home. My father-in-law, your grandpa Joey, was a very handy man. He could build walls and work with electricity as well as tackle any plumbing job. Well, he had built an apartment in the basement of their home, and that is where we laid our hats for a while. The plan was to save enough money to put down on a house before we moved. During the first five months, Michael attended baking school while I continued to work downtown. Our evenings were romantic with your dad usually making dinner. I would steal a kiss here and there before we finally retired in the living room to eat and watch TV. Afterward, we fell happily into each other's arms for the night.

When your father graduated, he acquired a job at a bakery but his hours were changed to the midnight shift. After a couple of weeks, we decided that was not going to work with us because we became like strangers passing in the night. He would be sleeping when I was awake and vice versa. I did not like sleeping alone anymore so I quit my job and got one with a 7-11 chain store working the same hours as he worked. The next year was crazy eating dinner by four in the afternoon and going to bed by six so we could get up by eleven to go to work.

However, we were your normal couple with our ups and downs. We did not always agree on things, and could accidentally upset each other. One time, I decided to take your father's motorcycle out for a ride on my own. I kicked up the stand and walked it out into the driveway. It was a lot heavier than I anticipated. When I tried to start it, the bike began to take off and fell sideways. It slid and I landed on the ground with my leg under it. I managed to get my leg out with just a few scrapes but I damaged the side mirror. I thought your dad was going to kill me! Yes, he had a temper being Italian, but so did I. We sure argued that day, and for a few hours neither one of us spoke. I hated it when we fought.

On another occasion, I made him spaghetti for dinner. I found a recipe book and followed it to a T. When I dished out the meal, I was so excited and proud of myself, but he rose from the table and told me that it was not the correct way to make Italian spaghetti sauce. He put his in the garbage and made himself a ham sandwich. My feelings were never so hurt. I cried for hours. Finally, he apologized for throwing out his dinner, and I vowed I would never make Italian food again. Before the end of the night, we always ended up lying in each other arms again.

Lisa, I just want you to know that just because you might argue or disagree with your partner, that does not mean you don't love each other. It's just a part of growing and maturing together.

Lisa felt some comfort with those words in the journal. It was nice to know that her parents did not always get along, but they knew they had something special and made every effort to keep it. She had some arguments with Joey and had quite a little temper herself. In fact, she could go on for a couple of days and ignore him when she was really angry. At those times even though she felt attracted to him, she was not sure if he was the man for her – the one with whom she would spend the rest of her life.

How do you really know? She wondered.

Lisa remembered the first time she met Joey with a group of kids at school that were all going to the movies. As they dispersed, she lagged behind since she did not feel like joining them. Joey noticed her standing alone and not following the group, so he asked her if she would like to get a milkshake or go somewhere to talk. She agreed, and to her surprise he took her to the Lincoln Park Zoo. They walked and looked at the animals in their small cages, which were so close together that they did not need to walk too far to see another one. They continued to walk and talk for hours while enjoying popcorn and cotton candy.

When they arrived at the house for the apes, he teased her saying that they were her family members looking at her through the glass. She didn't mind since it was all in good fun. Surprisingly, that small zoo offered plenty to see with a lion house, alligators, a reptile house, and a birdhouse just to name a few of its exhibits. It was a great way to break the ice, especially when they went into the children's zoo and were able to pet some animals. At the same time, they talked about everything from movies and music to their favorite stars. Lisa felt as if she had known him for years because he was so easy to talk with.

Joey admitted that he had seen her around, but needed to work up the courage to talk to her. That made her blush. After that day, he called her and met her after her classes so they could do their homework together. He told her a week later that he was in love with her, but did not expect her to feel the same way yet. However, he hoped given time that she would. It was difficult for Lisa to comprehend how Joey could know from just a week of talking with her that he was in love.

Where did the time go? Lisa wondered glancing at her watch.

It was already three in the afternoon. Her stomach made some noises, so she made her way downstairs to the kitchen. She opened the fridge door and found a bowl of chicken cacciatore that a neighbor had brought over. After she heated it up and ate it, she decided to clean the kitchen.

First she scrubbed out the fridge sorting what food was given the day of the funeral and what was old. The garbage can stunk from the old pieces of fruit and casserole bits that had mold on them. She took the garbage outside and used Mr. Clean to wash the shelves. The scent of spoiled food was soon replaced with a new fresh smell of cleanliness. Next she washed off the counter tops and the chandelier that hung over the kitchen table. The dust on the chandelier was a sure clue that her mother had not been herself during her final weeks. She had too much pride not to keep her house spotless. She then swept and washed the kitchen floor.

Time had gotten away from her, so Lisa decided to spend the night in her old room. She would be able to get an early start in the morning, but she felt a little lost. Perhaps in some way, she just needed to keep familiar things around. She just was not ready to leave, even though her parents were gone. Not to mention the fact that her mother had left her something to hang onto, and she absolutely had to finish reading her mother's wise words.

There was a knock at the front door that brought Lisa back to reality.

"Hi," said Joey, his long blond hair tied behind his back and a bouquet of daisies in his hands.

"Hi," Lisa replied walking out to the front steps.

What a wonderful surprise it was to see him. He leaned down to give her the sweetest kiss on the cheek and her heart pounded inside her chest.

"Do you feel like company?" He asked.

Lisa reached down, took his hand and led him into the house. She really felt the need to be with someone at that moment. She watched him as he strolled around looking at the pictures on the walls as if it were for the first time.

"You sure were a funny looking kid when you were growing up," he teased.

That put a smile on her face.

"Want to see the house?" She asked.

He nodded and followed her as they went from room to room. Joey had been there before, but she never really went through the whole house with him. He seemed interested as he looked at the markings by the bathroom wall. As they gazed upon her parents' wedding picture in the china cabinet, he commented on how handsome they looked. Then they went upstairs and she showed him her parents' room before she showed him her own. Lisa still found it a little unbelievable that the house belonged to her.

Joey walked around commenting on the animals and little love items that her parents had given to each other through the years.

"Your parents discovered true love, and I want the same thing one day," he said.

Lisa was a little old fashioned when it came to sex; she had not been with anyone yet. Even though she was in love with Joey, the right time had not yet presented itself. He looked at her room and sat on her bed so he could take in the wallpaper's planet pattern. Then he beckoned her to sit beside him. Immediately, she became nervous. Perhaps it was the way his eyes locked onto hers or how he whispered her name when he kissed her, telling her how much he loved her. That day marked the first time she ever made love. He was so natural and at ease, while she was scared. He was gentle with her and knew how to hold her, how and where to touch her, how to wait, and then how and when to just let everything on the inside explode. She loved the way he touched her, the gentle way he kissed her lips, her cheeks, her neck... well, everything.

"You are absolutely beautiful and you don't even know it, do you?" He asked sweetly.

His fingers stroked her face from her temple to her chin and she felt that all was right with the world. They lay in each other's arms until the sun came up. Then Joey had to leave for school. But before he did, he planted a deep kiss on her, which left her wanting more.

After he left and shut the front door, Lisa quickly ascended the stairs to her parents' room, jumped on the bed and opened the journal again.

Chapter Nine
A Love Story
Present Day - Crystal

"Mom, what a wonderful love story about grandma and grandpa," Crystal said with a yawn, "but how is this supposed to help me?"

"Patience, my dear," Lisa replied. "It's getting late. How about we get a good nights' sleep, and we'll continue in the morning. Make sure Blake knows you're spending the night so he doesn't worry."

"You know, Blake and I had a beautiful love story too... at one time."

Lisa helped her daughter up from the couch. They took their dishes into the kitchen and put them in the sink. It was one in the morning, and Crystal looked at her phone before closing her eyes to sleep. Yep, there was a text from Blake asking her what time she would be home. She sent him a short text back: **Not tonight.** Then she turned off her phone, closed her eyes, and tried to get comfortable so she could fall asleep, but tears quickly gathered in the back of her eyes. How she missed the way he used to look at her and kiss her when he got home from work.

What happened to make him so distant? She wondered.

She thought of her mother's story about her grandparents, and how happy they were so many years before. Thinking about that was a comforting way to fall asleep. As the sun rose, Crystal awoke and could smell coffee brewing in the kitchen. She threw on her robe and descended the stairs. When she walked into the kitchen, she caught a glimpse of her father.

"How's my baby girl doing?" Her father, Joey, asked planting a kissed on her forehead.

"We're both doing great, dad!" Crystal giggled holding her tummy.

She watched as her parents shared an embrace. She could feel the love between them. After her father left, Crystal quickly looked at her phone to see if there was a text from Blake. Nothing. She was a little angry with herself. She scrolled back to some of the old texts' they had shared before... One from Blake: **I love you and will be home soon.** One from her: **I love you, dinner is ready and I can't wait to see you.** She wanted to see a new text from him saying "I love you," but then she had not written one to him either.

As Crystal and her mother enjoyed coffee and toast, her mother pulled out the journal.

Chapter Ten
Being Pregnant
Natalie's Journal

Lisa, you should have seen how we scraped and saved. In a year and a half, we moved into our own home. We were both so busy. Your dad tiled the floor by the front door, and I planted flowers outside around the house. We painted and wallpapered together, and it was great. What better way to show our love for each other than to fix up our own home? I never thought I could be so happy. What a sense of accomplishment when you do something with your spouse that is so beautiful and meaningful to both of you.

Then the inevitable happened. I felt sick one day, you know, like I had the flu. I stayed in bed that day throwing up, unable to eat. The following day, I felt better but still nauseous and tired. This feeling lasted about a week, so I decided to call the doctor. That was when I found out I was pregnant with you. We were still so young. I was twenty-one, and your father was twenty-three. Of all the things we talked about, we never discussed children. I mean we said someday we wanted a boy and a girl, but we were just into each other and thought children were in the far future. When I told your father I was pregnant, it took him by surprise.

"I still feel sick," I told him.

"You really need to eat something, sweetie," he replied staring at my green face.

He decided to make me scrambled eggs. I could hear the spatula in the pan as he swirled the eggs around, but it was the smell that got to me first. He raised the pan and poured the eggs on the plate placing the plate in front of me, and I immediately ran to the bathroom! Your father chased after me looking worried.

"You okay?" he asked holding me firmly about my waist.

There I was on the floor hugging the toilet not sure of what I should do.

"You need to see the doctor," he insisted.

I took his advice and made an appointment for the following day. After a few questions, a urine sample, and some blood tests the doctor gave me his diagnosis. When I arrived back home, Michael had just finished making us dinner. He kissed me gently on the lips and asked what the doctor had said. I just blurted it out, "I'm pregnant."

He was quiet at first. He kept repeating over and over, "How can that be? You were on the pill?"

He was not mad or happy. He was simply confused because children had not even been considered at that time. I started to cry. I could tell that he was bothered by my news. Finally, he wrapped his arms around me and held me close. Then, he pushed me back to look into my eyes.

"I guess we're going to be parents!" He said with a grin, and we hugged again.

I was so relieved to hear that, and knew right then and there that we would be great parents. From that point on, we simply took life as it came, and boy did it come fast! We were busier than ever as we put all of our energy into creating a cute nursery room for you. I wanted little teddy bears as the theme, and we found wallpaper with them on it. In between them were tiny rattles. We put the paper on one wall and painted the others yellow, green, and blue since we didn't know if you would be a boy or a girl.

My parents held a baby shower for me, and I received all sorts of little buntings, T-shirts, and receiving blankets. You have no idea how cute the little garments look when you're pregnant. I picked up one of the socks and wondered if anyone can have feet that small. My in-laws bought me the sweetest white crib with a bedspread displaying teddy bears on it. I found this big teddy bear and placed it in the corner of your crib, and your father brought home an adorable mobile with teddy bears on it that played, "It's A Small World After All."

I wasn't sure I liked the idea of getting a big waistline and having to wear the larger clothes. However, the most thrilling part of being pregnant was hearing your heart beat for the first time. The second was feeling you kicking inside of me. I remember the first time your father felt you kick. You were just so active that day, and I could not get comfortable. Your dad asked me why I could not sit still. Finally, I put his hand on my stomach. He watched and felt it move as you stretched inside of me. He couldn't believe that you were alive in there having a party as he put it.

Labor pains are not fun and delivering a baby definitely does hurt. Don't believe anyone who says differently! Just remember that it's only one day of pain, and the rest of your life will be joyful with your child. Finally, you arrived and were very much loved. It was hard for me to understand how your dad and I could make such a perfect little girl. And I didn't know how anyone could not believe in God with the miracle of life that we had created together. When I held you for the first time, you looked straight at me as if saying, "Hi, I finally get to meet you mom." Your tiny finger was wrapped around mine. You would just nurse and fall asleep like you had always belonged here. Your dad was ecstatic, and couldn't help bragging about you at work. To watch you hold your head up for the first time and then to see you sit up and eventually crawl, everything was so exciting for me. So that was our new life with you. Again, I never thought I could be happier than I was at that wonderful time with your dad and you.

I quit my job and was a stay-at-home mom. It was a little harder financially, but we both agreed that we wanted to raise you, not a day care. My days were filled with diapers, nursing, and taking you on walks in your buggy. To hold your little body close to mine while you nursed was so rewarding, and I knew we were forming what would become a life-long connection with each other. I used to watch the rhythm of your little chest move while you slept in your crib, which brought tears to my eyes. To hear you say mama and dada was unbelievable. You were so smart! You walked by ten months old, and I had trouble keeping up with you. Of course, your dad was also in love with you. He couldn't wait to see you when you got up in the morning. Sometimes, I gave you a bottle even when you didn't really need it just so he could feed you instead of me.

We had this big party for your first birthday, and naturally you don't remember, but everyone was there - your grandpas and grandmas, relatives and neighbors. I made a teddy bear cake, as well as a cupcake just for you. We put your little finger into the icing and brought it to your lips. It took you a couple of minutes to taste it, but when you did you picked up the cupcake and smashed it into your face. I think that's when you discovered you had a sweet tooth!

Lisa put the journal down, and went into her mother's closet. She wanted to find the photo album with the pictures of her first birthday party. When she did, she reclined back on her mothers' bed. However, her mother's memories prompted her to look back to that time through pictures when everyone looked so happy. She laughed aloud when she saw how funny she looked with all that icing on her face. As she scanned the photos, she could see that her parents were very happy during the first year of her life. There was one with her as a tiny baby sleeping in her mother's arms. There was another of her father smiling and kissing her on the cheek. When she reached one with her dressed in a mouse costume, she knew it must have been her first Halloween. She chuckled aloud at the little whiskers that her mom put on her face, and the big ears on her head.

There were pictures of her first Christmas with Grandpa Joe dressed as Santa Claus and holding her while she cried. She could tell by the many photos that both sets of grandparents loved her dearly. There were many where they held and kissed her. All of them gave her a sense of peace. Flipping through the pages, she watched herself grow up in front of her parent's eyes, if only her mom could have been sitting there with them to enjoy those memories. Her eyes grew heavy and before she knew it, she opened up her eyes with the sun shining on her face. She had fallen asleep in such a good mood dreaming of herself as a baby with the picture album on the pillow next to her head, and the journal lying on the bed. Smiling she sat up and began to read again.

Your dad was still working the midnight shift. I took care of you during the day and slept at night without him, making it difficult for us to have intimate time together. I suppose that's how it is whenever a new baby is born, but wouldn't you know it, by the time you were two, I was pregnant again. Now, I know this is going to be hard for you because you were too small for me to tell you about anything at the time. Please don't be angry with me and try to understand as I attempt to explain.

When I told your father I was pregnant, I'm not sure that he was as happy as me. Once I experienced motherhood, I didn't want it to stop. What I wanted more than anything in the world was to be a mother again. I enjoyed taking care of you and I thought I had enough love inside of me for more, but to him I think it meant a larger financial burden on his shoulders. Don't think for a minute that he thought you were a burden, because he loved you very much. He just had trouble figuring out how to pay the bills with only one paycheck, and then there would be another mouth to feed.

That pregnancy started out like it did with you; I was sick at first and extremely tired. I couldn't wait to take naps with you. I still hadn't lost all the weight from having you so I think that's why I started showing even faster than the first time, but I didn't care. I was so proud, and felt so lucky to be pregnant again.

One of the fun things you and I did was go to the Museum of Science and Industry to check out the prenatal development center, where there were human fetuses in various sizes of bottles. We would return each month so I could see how much my baby had grown, which made me feel closer to my unborn child. Of course you really didn't care about all that. You much preferred to walk through the giant heart on display and hear it beating. Well, you know we liked the museum since we returned often until you were in high school.

I was in the beginning of my fifth month and felt a sharp pain one day above my uterus. You and your father were in the living room watching television, and I was cleaning the dinner dishes. The pain felt like a stabbing knife and quite literally took my breath away. I figured it was just Braxton Hicks, contractions that don't represent true labor, so I knelt down on the floor and took slow breaths until it went away. I didn't bother telling anyone because a lot of women get those false labor pains. While we were getting ready for bed that night, the unbearable pain returned. I doubled over and your father heard me moan.

"What's wrong?" he asked.

I saw the worried look on his face, and I wanted to calm him down so I told him it was nothing. However, the pain returned again and with blood that time. Your father quickly sprang into action. He called his parents to come and get you before he helped me into the car and drove me to the hospital. By the time we arrived, I felt a lot better and they brought me to the delivery floor. They decided to monitor me since I did have some bleeding. They took my vitals and then told me that something was wrong. My blood pressure was too high, which posed a danger for both the baby and me. Next, they put a baby monitor on me, but they couldn't hear a heartbeat. My own heart missed a beat when I heard that. I prayed over and over again that God would not let my baby die and before I knew it. I was being prepped for surgery. I was told that I had to have an emergency C-section, but that your father would have to stay in the waiting room. I could see the sadness on his face when he leaned down to kissed me goodbye.

"It'll be all right," I assured. "They'll take good care of our baby and me."

Then everything started to move quickly as an IV was inserted in my arm. I was rolled into the operating room and was lying on the table. I could feel my belly being scrubbed to prepare me for the surgery. At the same time, they were still trying to hear the baby's heart, but with no success.

"Oh God," I prayed. "Please let my baby be all right."

An oxygen mask was placed over my face. I tried to push it off, but the medical staff was stronger. All I remember after that was falling into pitch darkness. I thought I was dying, and I remember apologizing to the baby for leaving him. Yes you guessed it; you would have had a brother. I guess I was knocked out, because what I remembered next was a woman slapping my face to wake me up. Everything was a blur at first. I saw this red bag of blood hanging over my head, and felt a pair of prongs in my nose. When I finally awoke, I yelled to anyone who would listen that I wanted to see my baby. The nurse told me to calm down, but would not tell me what happened. Eventually, another nurse entered the room with something wrapped up in a blue blanket. This baby was so small, Lisa. I probably could have held him in one hand and still have some room left over. The nurse gently uncovered him and opened his legs to let me see that my baby was a boy. Tears streamed down my face, Lisa. All I could think of was whether God was punishing me?

While she read the pages, Lisa's mind became muddled with so many questions. For the rest of the day, she was full of confusion. *I had a baby brother... but he died? Why didn't anyone tell me? Oh sure, I was too young at the time but what about later in life? Did my parents think I wouldn't understand that it wasn't their fault?*

Lisa recalled the many trips to the museum over the years, and how much she really enjoyed that place.

She wondered if the fact that her mother could watch the baby growing inside of her caused her to love it so much. Then she remembered the summer before her freshman year in high school. Her mom had begged her to go to the museum with a promise that she wouldn't make her go once she entered the high school doors. Lisa had always enjoyed Colleen Moore's Fairy Castle and taking rides in the coal mine, but there was something else. She recalled one time when her mother made a special trip to see the fetuses on the third floor in the glass jars. She only walked up to one that was twenty-four weeks old.

"Mom, what's wrong?" Lisa had asked.

Her mom just stared at it holding a Kleenex to her eyes. She made a little muffled cry before she blew her nose.

"Nothing, sweetie," she said. "I think I am getting a cold."

But even as a child, Lisa could see that her mother was trembling.

"Come on, mom. We have so much more to see," she said pulling her by the hand.

That was the last time they ever went there.

How could I have known that there was this big secret and mom was revisiting something awful from her past?

Lisa needed time to digest what she had just learned. She felt the best way to deal with something as shocking as that was to keep busy. She pulled out the vacuum and headed to the carpet in the living room, followed by the family room, and then to do the wash downstairs. When she realized that she was using work to keep things off her mind, it reminded her all the more of her mother. Her mom always said that cleaning the house would comfort her, and let her mind rest.

Later that evening Joey called. He wanted to come over, but Lisa had too much still rattling around in her brain and wasn't sure that having company would be a good idea. She did want to talk to him, but felt it would be easier to do so on the phone. Pity was the last thing she wanted to see in his eyes. She told him about the brother that she almost had, and speaking out loud about his death made her cry. She had not even known him, yet she cried for him. Lisa wasn't sure if she should be mad at her mother for not telling her, but that seemed rather pointless, since her mom had died too. Death was becoming the word she dreaded the most.

How can it be that you go through twenty years of life without experiencing death, and then in a matter of weeks everyone you love has gone?

Talking to Joey did make her feel better, and part of her almost wished she had asked him to come over, but after having some hot soup and climbing into her bed with the afghan that her mother had made, she fell instantly asleep. Morning came fast and for Lisa, it was a brand new day. She felt refreshed and ready to focus again on the journal.

Lisa settled on her parents' bed and continued to read.

Lisa, this is going to be the hardest part of the journal for you to read, but you have to understand the circumstances. I am not making excuses for our actions, but we are human and do make mistakes. First, I was not doing very well after the miscarriage. I cried all the time. I had trouble losing the extra weight, and I grew more and more depressed. I didn't put on makeup anymore. I just didn't seem to care about anything except you. I wasn't there for your dad. Of course, I felt like he wasn't there for me either. He finally got mad at me for crying so much, so I would wait until the both of you were asleep, creep into the living room, and I'd sit on the couch and sob into a pillow. I cried hard screaming at God, and asking Him why he was punishing me. Sometimes my throat hurt because I cried so much, and my eyes seemed to stay puffy. Lisa, I really felt like I was being punished for some reason, but I didn't understand why.

Losing a baby was the most horrible experience in the world. To see the child that I was carrying so small and not breathing was horrific. What was wrong with me? Did I not eat a proper diet or did I not rest enough? Did I stretch too high when I washed the kitchen walls? Was I a bad person so God decided that I did not deserve this gift? Yes, I believe that children are gifts, and you, my dear, were the best gift that God ever gave me.

Your father took the death differently. He felt as if it were meant to be. If that was what God wanted, then I should be okay with it too. It would be financially better for us. Even though we still had the hospital bill, at least he did not have another mouth to feed. He just could not understand why I was so downhearted and sad.

That's when it started. The phone calls from your father at work became less and less. His hours were strange and he always arrived home at different times. Finally one day, he came home and went straight into the bedroom to sleep, which quickly became a habit.

We seemed to stop communicating, no touching, nothing. I was so depressed that I grew angry with him for not spending time with us. He seemed so indifferent that he just stopped talking. I was caught in my own world of depression and could not understand why your father wasn't there for me.

I am not sure I really noticed that he wasn't around so much until one day when you and I spent the night at my parents' home. Your father had to work, so you and I went for the weekend alone. I needed a break from him anyway. My parents tried to console me as I still cried over losing the baby. They reminded me of how lucky I was to have you. I needed the comfort of their kind words, and the comfort of hugs.

Finally on Sunday night, I kissed my parents goodbye and drove home feeling a little better about everything. I even thought I needed to try to make things up with your father. After all, it takes two to fight. I brought you into the quiet house and you started calling for your father. He came out to greet us and when I leaned in to give him a kiss on the cheek, he seemed shy. We had not kissed each other in a while so I figured I would make the first move to restart the intimacy again.

"Hey," I said to Michael. "I missed you."

He slowly drew up a small smile before he said he missed me too, but something definitely felt a little different to me about the way he acted. My intuition told me that something was wrong. I did not like the way that felt at all. We went to bed together and for the first time in a long time, I longed for him to make love to me. His lips quivered when he kissed me and he did not take the time that he usually did. I was not sure who he was at that moment. I felt like I really didn't know him. I turned on my side of the bed and moved my pillow, I had a panic attack. I did not know what to do or how to approach what I saw. My body broke out in a cold sweat and I could hardly breathe. There on the sheets was some dry beige foundation of makeup. My heart started beating so fast that I had to get out of there. I tripped when I got out of the bed and fell to the floor. Your father woke up startled by the sudden commotion

"Come back to bed, Natalie," he said in a sleepy voice.

I could not believe it. He acted like nothing happened.

"Michael!" I shouted. My face turned red and my eyes opened wide enough to shoot daggers. I could tell by his face that he had no idea what I was upset about.

"What's the problem," he asked bewildered.

I did not know what to say. Since I could not say it, I just pointed to the stain on the sheets.

"So you forgot to take off your makeup," he laughed. "It will wash."

How stupid did he think I was?

"I don't wear makeup to bed, Michael," I replied.

I rushed out of the bedroom and into the night air. I had to walk or even run. I had to think. I had trouble comprehending what was going on, but one thing was sure: my husband was having an affair. I walked quickly for a couple of miles before I returned home. I cried and prayed asking God what was happening. I was so angry and hurt that I had to get some of the anxiety out of my system. What was I supposed to do then? How much more was I able to take? My head hurt along with the muscles of my legs as I continued to walk briskly. With unanswered questions and feeling so tired, I made my way back up the walk to our house. I must have slammed the door; I don't remember, but I heard you crying so I went to your room to see what was wrong. You looked up at me with such sad eyes as if in some strange way, you knew I was hurting. I picked you up and sat with you on the rocking chair.

"I'm here sweetie," I whispered. "I'm here, right here and I'm not going anywhere. I'll always be here for you."

I needed you at that moment as much as you needed me. We rocked back and forth until your eyes closed and I could feel your body grow heavy with sleep. That's when I remembered what my mother told me.

"Life does not go on forever, Natalie. Enjoy every moment that you're given this gift," she said.

Chapter Thirteen
Questions
Present Day - Crystal

"Mom," cried Crystal, "you mean to tell me that grandpa cheated on grandma? And you wanted to share this with me?"

Crystal openly expressed her anger with the feeling that all men were scum. Well, all men except her dad, of course.

"How is that supposed to help my husband and me?" She questioned.

"Patience, my dear," she said. "You have to let me finish the story."

The baby started to kick, and Crystal had trouble getting comfortable. It really hurt when his little feet ran up and down her ribs. She wished that she could put the big belly on a shelf for a couple of hours just to have a break. Time was passing quickly and she knew that very soon, she would finally have her baby.

"How about taking a nice long bath before I continue," her mother suggested. "And please don't make any judgments about your grandparents until I finish."

"Deal," said Crystal, "but I'm entitled to my own opinion."

In the bathroom the warm water was just what Crystal needed. It seemed to settle the baby down and relaxed her, but her mind did not stop. All she could think about was Blake – how she missed him yet at the same time, how angry she was with him.

Why can't he understand that it's uncomfortable enough being ready to pop a baby out? She wondered. *Was it her fault that sometimes she grew short tempered?* Most of the time she felt so uncomfortable, and seldom had a good night's sleep. Okay, so he told her that his company was sold and he had a new boss. She also saw how Katherine looked at her husband when she was introduced to her. She was at least ten years older than Crystal, well-endowed with a cute figure, and wore bright red lipstick.

Well, anyone right now would have a better figure than me! She thought. *I'm just so fat, but what hurts the most is the way he smiled back at Katherine...*

After her bath, she joined her mother in the living room, ready to hear more about her cheating grandpa.

Chapter Fourteen
The Past
Lisa's Story Continues

The first time Lisa read about her father's infidelity, she was alone in her bedroom. She became so angry that she dropped the journal to the floor, took her fist, and slammed it against her thigh. She jumped off the bed, ran to the closet, and one at a time grabbed her father's clothes off the hangers throwing them onto the floor. She was so confused; her head was full of so many flashing thoughts that it began to hurt. To comprehend that her father had an affair just did not set right with her. Dress shirts, play shirts, dress pants, shorts, even his suits were all thrown with deliberate force to the middle of the closet floor. Next she grabbed his shoes and threw them on top of the clothes until the shelves were clear. The hangers were empty, and all she could see hanging were her mother's clothes.

She tried to remember how old she must have been when her father cheated on her mother. *Probably three years old, maybe four...* she speculated. She'd have to do the math, *but why did that even matter?* That was another thing her parents never told her. *Why didn't mom leave him?* She wondered. *Why was dad not loyal to us? Yes to us! Whatever he did, he did it to both of us.* It was difficult to comprehend that it was her father, the loving man she grew up with, that did such an unforgivable thing and hurt the both of them. She tried hard to think back in time, but could not recall a situation when he seemed indifferent to her.

She grew angrier as she questioned why her mom even wrote the journal. Then she remembered what her mother had said just a few weeks before when she was encouraged to remember the nice things about her father. *Why did she write this if she just wanted me to recall good things about my dad?* Lisa needed to get away. She ran down the stairs to the kitchen, picked up the phone, and dialed.

"Hello?" Said the masculine voice on the other end.

"Joey, I need to get out of here. Can you come and pick me up?" She asked weakly.

"Is everything all right?" He asked. "Of course I'll come. Give me a few, and I'll be right over."

"Thanks," she said, and hung up the phone.

If there were anyone she could depend on, it would be Joey. Exhausted from all the energy she expended, she slowly climbed the stairs and got dressed for the day. What she needed was a day out – a day with Joey, the man she loved. She needed to get out of the shadow of her parents, and back into reality.

When Joey arrived, she fell into him crying. He saw how upset she was and decided to help get her mind off things. Silently with only the radio and Lisa's whimpers, he drove downtown. He took her to the John Hancock building, and they went up the elevator to the cafe. There was something so beautiful about looking down at the city from so high up. The cars looked like tinker toys, plus you could see that some of the apartments had pools on top of them. So many buildings with so many different heights, it looked very crowded. And to see the Lake Michigan shoreline was beautiful as well. She held his hand tightly as they took a seat by the window. Just looking down at the city offered a comforting feeling.

"Hungry?" He asked as the waiter placed the menus on the table.

"No," she whispered and then sighed loudly.

She actually felt better already. Joey ordered them some burgers and cokes, and waited patiently for Lisa to tell him what had happened.

"Joey," she said finally with a sniffle, "I just found out my dad had an affair."

She peered into his eyes searching for an answer. He did not say anything and his face remained calm.

"Did you hear what I said?" She continued.

"And what does that have to do with you or me?" He asked shrugging his shoulders.

Tears filled her eyes again and her mouth twitched as she tried not to let them fall.

"Your parents seemed happy enough. I think your mom must have forgiven him."

"We were betrayed," she said as a couple of tears slipped down her cheeks. "How could he do that?"

Joey put his arms around her for comfort, something she really needed at that time. She fell into his body and held him close.

"You know I love you, don't you?" He whispered in her ear.

Lisa shook her head but kept her face dug into his shoulder.

"That will never happen with us."

She wanted to believe that so badly, but her dad, whom she loved so much and seemed like a family man, had strayed. *How could she be sure that Joey wouldn't do the same thing? If she could not trust her own father, how could she trust any other man?*

They ate in silence while the view from the tall building caused her mind to sway to other things. The wonderful view took over as if to say all is well. Look at the good and don't hold on to the bad.

"Beautiful isn't it," Lisa said quietly between bites.

"Not as beautiful as you," Joey replied with a wink.

Her heart jumped an extra beat. That was what she needed to hear. She needed Joey and his love to comfort her. They spent the rest of the day together and she talked him into going to the Museum of Science and Industry, reliving her past with her mother. They went into the Coal Mine, down the old cobblestone street and watched a classic silent movie before entering Finnegan's Ice Cream Parlor. After enjoying a sundae, they headed up to the third floor. They walked through the human heart trying not to get run over by children playing in there, and then Lisa led Joey to the prenatal development area. She held his hand and scanned all the human fetuses. At the one that said twenty-four weeks, she stopped and he could feel her body begin to shake.

"What's wrong?" He asked pulling her close with his arm around her waist.

He looked at all the fetuses in the glass bottles and thought perhaps Lisa just could not bear seeing the dead babies.

"I'm sure they were already dead before they were put in those glass cages," he noted. "It's kind of freaky, isn't it? They probably had to get permission and they are useful as teaching tools."

Lisa tried to stop the tears as they gathered in the back of her eyes.

"See that one?" She asked. "That's how big my brother was when he was born."

"I'm sorry, Lisa. I didn't know."

They stood quietly for a moment with only the noise of the children running around the museum ringing in their ears. Joey never let her go, squeezing her waist to let her know he was there for her. He did not rush her and when she was ready to leave, he followed her. They drove home in silence with the radio playing soft music and each of them lost in their own private worlds.

"Are you all right?" He asked as he turned into the driveway.

Lisa looked up at him with thankful eyes.

"Can you stay with me tonight?" She asked softly.

He smiled and kissed her before helping her out of the car.

"I think they're playing our song," he said playfully and twirled her around toward the porch.

Her heart jumped with delight; he knew how to make her smile. They danced into the house and Joey put on the radio. They continued to dance slowly in the living room. Holding her tightly, Lisa could feel the comfort needed to get through that tough day. She followed his lead as they danced and then his lips found hers. They made their way to her bedroom and made love before falling asleep. It was a magical night that she'd never forget.

Chapter Fifteen
A Struggle with Infidelity
Natalie's Journal

Lisa, I know you must be having a difficult time reading this, but you must not stop. Please don't let your anger toward your father for what he did take hold of your heart or think any bad thoughts of him. Hopefully in the end, you will understand.

The next day I kicked your father out of our house. I did not have to think twice about it. I did not think I deserved what he did, and he did not deserve to be with us due to his betrayal. And he didn't even argue with me, as if he knew I was right. He immediately packed his bags and moved back home with his parents. Of course, they were devastated, and my parents were angry. It's amazing how one person can upset so many more. It definitely had a domino effect.

Lisa, I don't know if I can put into words how I felt at that time - betrayed, abandoned, and double-crossed I suppose. My heart was so broken. I know the word hate is a very strong one to use, but I was not sure if I was actually capable of hating even then. It's kind of funny how life can change a person and show a side of you that you did not know existed. For example, I would never have guessed in a thousand years that your father would cheat on me. What could I do with that? Part of me urged me to say good-bye forever. I was young and if I lost about ten pounds, I knew I could catch another man – one that would never, ever think of being disloyal to me. What could I have done wrong to cause him to be unfaithful? Part of me felt like a failure. Was I not attentive enough? Was I not pretty enough? But was that what love was about? Didn't he understand that what he did was wrong? My mind was out of control.

My head ached and I had no appetite, but I tried so hard to be there for you. All I did was cry and you grew crabby too, but I knew it was because my attention was not as much on you as it should have been. I didn't blame you. It was my fault.

I called the pastor that married us and told him on the phone the short version of what had happened. He just listened as I rattled on between tears, and then he asked me if I would come in to see him. The only problem was that he did not have an appointment available for another week. It seemed so far away but I truly needed to talk to someone who was not biased. The week passed slowly as I continued to take care of you. Meanwhile, your father called me every day, but I ignored him.

"Natalie," Pastor Clem said as I entered the church office and shook his hand, "so good to see you." He was at least as old as my father with a head of gray hair, and a little tummy that hung over his belt.

I smiled, but was terrified inside. Should I tell the pastor what happened? Would he even understand? We had talked on the phone, but he wanted to know everything from the beginning. I explained about the little boy I lost, and how it seemed at that time that I could feel a growing distance with your father. I told him again about the makeup I found on the bed sheets. My body was shaking, and I began to cry. The pastor handed me a tissue, and I blew my nose before continuing. When I finally finished, he just sat back and shook his head.

"There is no reason for you to stay with someone who has been unfaithful," he began.

The pastor walked around the room with his eyes closed and his hands folded behind his back. I could hear his feet shuffle on the floor with slow steps, and then I heard him sniffle before he went on.

"God did not put a couple together to hurt each other, and he definitely does not approve of cheating."

I lifted my eyes toward him and stiffened my back forward.

What's he trying to say, I wondered? Does he think I should divorce Michael? Would a pastor of a church really tell me that?

I felt terribly confused, and my chest began to hurt. I was still in love with your father. I was so devastated by all that had occurred that I didn't know what to think. Pastor Clem rubbed the crease on his forehead and sat down next to me.

"Let me tell you a story, Natalie."

I noticed his eyes turning red and he quickly dabbed them with some Kleenex.

"Being a pastor, I hear all sorts of stories. I see all kinds of people. I minister to so many, and I'm on call twenty-four hours a day. I go to nursing homes and hospitals to visit the sick and elderly. That's not counting the phone calls I receive from hurting people

who need advice from me because I'm a servant of the Lord and should have all the correct answers for them."

I watched as his body began to shake and tears fell down his cheeks. I was not sure what he had to say, but I could see it was very painful for him to go on, yet he did.

"One day when I went home, my wife had her suitcase packed," he said breathing deeply. "She told me she was leaving me. She said I was not home enough for her needs. She said that everyone was more important than her, and she didn't have to live that way. She wanted a man who loved her and wanted to be around her more often."

I watched as his body trembled with each word from his mouth.

"You see, I was so busy helping other people that I wasn't there for her. I did not even realize that I had placed her on the back burner. I just had so many people that needed me. Well, we talked, and we prayed, and she gave me a second chance. "

I could not believe he was telling me something so personal. I tried to understand what that had to do with me. I was there for my husband. I did not have another job; I was a stay-at-home mother. And I did not cheat on my husband.

"I didn't do anything wrong," I blurted out. "You said so yourself."

"No you didn't, Natalie," Pastor Clem said, "but did I do something that was so terribly wrong that my wife wanted to leave me?"

I searched his face for a clue as to what he meant.

"You were helping other people, Pastor Clem. Why would she be so mad about that?"

"But I wasn't there for her needs, Natalie." He paused for a few moments and then asked, "In the Bible does it say that one sin is worse than another?"

I must have had a weird expression on my face as if I did not understand.

"You know what I mean. Is it worse to kill, steal, or lie? You see, Natalie, I had to correct the way I was thinking. I needed to put God first, my wife second, and my job third. Your husband is still in training, and only if you let him, he can have a second chance too – a chance to make things right. Perhaps you can find it in your heart to show him God's love. If you can forgive him, you could be an example of God's love, and show him the right path."

What's he trying to say? I wondered. Does the pastor expect me to act like nothing ever happened?

My head spun as I listened to his words. By that time, tears poured down his face.

"You didn't deserve what he did to you, and no one would think ill of you if you left him. You have every right to do that, if that is your wish. However, I remember the last words I said to the both of you on your wedding day. What God has put together let no man take apart. If you decide to stay to show God's love and forgiveness, what a witness you could be."

We knelt and said a prayer together before he sent me home. I was never as confused as I was at that time. That night so many thoughts raced through my mind. I was still so angry and hurt. Could I really forgive your father? I never even considered that. I took out the card the pastor gave me before I left and read it.

'Love is patient; love is kind. It does not envy; it does not boast; it is not proud; it does not dishonor others; it is not self-seeking; it is not easily angered; it keeps no record of wrongs. Love does not delight in evil, but rejoices with the truth. It always protects, always trusts, always hopes; always perseveres.'

I remember when he read that at our wedding. We also said in sickness and in health till death do us part. I was getting a learning lesson on life, Lisa. No, I did nothing wrong, but maybe I really was doing something wrong. Was I being patient or kind? Was I not keeping a record of his wrong-doings?

Lisa, I still could not talk to your father when I got home. I went on through the next week taking care of you, still crying and not eating. I lost ten pounds in two weeks. I felt as if I had the good angel and the bad angel on each of my shoulders. One would tell me to leave him, not give him another chance. He did not deserve it and I was young enough to find happiness for the rest of my life. The good angel reminded me of my wedding vows, and that there was nothing wrong with giving someone a second chance. That one kept ringing in my head because of what Pastor Clem said about being an example for God. But what if I gave him another chance and he did the same thing again? Finally I broke down, called your father and told him we needed to talk. I had to understand what was going on... so we planned a date.

Chapter Sixteen
Good Memories
Lisa's Story Continues

It was Sunday morning when Lisa was reading the journal in her parents' room. She usually went to church with her parents but once she got into college, she missed a lot of Sundays by using the excuse that she had papers to finish. She put the journal down trying to digest what her mom had written.

She thought of her friends at school, and when a boyfriend would cheat. They said the first time was shame on him and the second time – shame on you. She was never going to let someone use her like that. She always figured that if Joey cheated on her, she would be gone like a flash of lightening. Yet her thoughts of him were so familiar and happy. He was her best friend and made her feel good. He was smart and never pushy. He was also so handsome with his long blond hair. He seemed to know when to talk and when to just be there for her, but her mother put this in such different terms. It was as if this life was a lesson in learning where we could all make mistakes, and we should be capable of giving or accepting apologies along with a second chance.

It was difficult for her to imagine her father with someone else, and her mother so angry and even full of hatred. Her mother was the kindest person she had ever known. Her memories were only good ones with plenty of laughter and love between them.

Lisa remembered the time she visited a nursing home with her mother and talked to some of the old people. Her mother had made chocolate chip cookies and passed them around as she said hello. It seemed the older folks liked having a young person visit. They didn't even mind Lisa wheeling them around in the halls. It was scary at first, and the smell was not very nice, but her mom told her that everyone needed a friend sometimes so she tried to be nice and everyone accepted her.

Lisa decided to call her grandparents – her father's parents – and they were delighted to hear from her. With both of her parents gone, she needed to be with them, to feel the warmth and comfort of family around her. As she dialed their number, she wondered if she should ask them about what her mother had written. Time with them would tell.

"Is everything all right?" Asked Grandma Jean.

"Yeah, I just miss you guys. I want to come over and visit if you don't mind."

"You know you're always welcome, Lisa," she said. "We're always happy to see you."

Lisa jumped into the car and drove to their home. Her grandparents were in their seventies, still with minds intact and able to walk around with only a few aches and pains to joints. Grandma Jean had brown hair that she maintained with a little help from Miss Clairol. She was always busy cooking and working in her garden. Grandpa Joe was totally bald, had a belly, and was such a wiz with automobiles. He was always helping the neighbors with their car engines. She wondered if her dad would have been bald if he had made it to that age.

When Lisa arrived, Grandma Jean had a pot roast cooking, which gave her that old familiar smell of home. Of course, the carrots and potatoes in the pot were from her garden. After hugs hello from grandma and grandpa they pulled out their photo albums, settled on the couch, and went back in time reminiscing about when her dad was a little boy. Lisa could see her face in her father Michaels' when he was a child. They told her once when he was three years old, they thought they lost him, and it took a couple of hours to find him. He had a cute brown haired dog and that day, he decided to take a nap in the doghouse. If it weren't for the dog waking up and barking to get their attention, they would not have found him until he woke up.

They talked about old times such as the day Michael first played ball in the backyard and broke the window to the back door with his fastball pitch. And the time someone tried to take his lunch money and he got expelled from school for fighting. That day also marked her father's first black eye. Lisa saw how her grandparents' eyes beamed as they bragged about their son. Grandpa Joe told her about her father taking guitar lessons and how proud he was of Michael when he heard him play.

"Did you know that your father sold his guitar and amplifier to buy your mother her engagement ring?" Grandpa Joe asked.

Lisa shook her head no, thinking that was so romantic.

"Yeah, your father was so in love with your mother. He married her right away so no one else would have a chance to get to know her."

Then he pulled out her parents' wedding pictures.

"See how beautiful your mother was?" He asked.

A tear ran down Grandma Jean's cheek as she relived her son's wedding. Lisa had seen the pictures before, but it was so refreshing to hear how happy they were when her dad married her mother. All Lisa could think of was that she wanted to be that happy when she got married.

Next came pictures of Lisa as a baby. Her grandparents could not express enough how beautiful she was, and how proud they were of her.

"The day you were born, I cried with your other grandmother at this beautiful baby girl that we were going to be able to spoil," Grandma Jean said. "Your mother was not sure what to do the first week you were home. You cried so much and she was so frustrated. I told her to relax, that you could feel her anxiousness, and that was why you kept crying."

She stopped for a moment and smiled admiring the pictures.

"Your mother was a good mom and caught on fast about how to take care of you. It would be so easy if babies came with a step by step manual!"

Lisa could not help laughing along with her grandmother.

"You know, your mother called me the day you sat up all by yourself. She was giggling on the phone and so proud of you," she said. "She had so much fun putting ribbons in your hair and putting you in lacy dresses."

Lisa did not think she could ever feel any better than she did reliving her past through her grandparents.

"Then she was so elated when you took your first step," her grandma continued. "Your dad took such great pride in how fast you learned to do these things."

"Yeah, but that didn't last long," Grandpa Joe laughed. "You got into everything. You were a little tomboy, and the dresses just got in the way."

Lisa really needed to hear all of that. She felt like her parents were in the same room while she listened to her grandparents stories. It was fun reliving growing up in her grandparents eyes. Yet she was confused as to why no one brought up the fact that her dad cheated on her mom. They had such lovely things to say about both her parents she wasn't sure how to approach the subject. Had they forgiven him and let the past go?

"Grandma, wasn't there a time when my parents were not getting along?" Lisa asked. Grandma Jean's eyes opened wide and her smile disappeared.

"Yes my dear," she managed to say. "I didn't know you knew." She paused for a second gathering her thoughts. "Your father strayed and hurt your mother very bad. He came back here to live with us, and we were so disappointed in him, that we could not even talk at first." A couple of tears slid down her cheeks. "Those are the dark days that we try to forget." She said as she took her hand and smoothed down the hair on Lisa's head. "Your father went to work and moped around the house, he missed your mother so much. But worse of all, he was having trouble forgiving himself. He needed to hear your mom say the magic words, I forgive you."

"It took a few weeks but then your mother called him and they talked." She continued. "After their talk he packed his bags and went back home. I don't think

I have ever seen two people more in love. Your mother showed him forgiveness and love. She taught all of us about the power of love as she took him back."

"You know, Lisa," Grandpa Joe said, "Sometimes life does not go the way we think it should, and we have to make life decisions that will affect us for the rest of our lives." He took Grandma Jeans hand and gave it a squeeze. "We are so proud of both of your parents. They figured out how to have a happy life as they forgave any wrong doings."

Grandma Jean picked up a picture of Michael, Natalie, and Lisa. Lisa watched the smile grow on her grandfathers' face, and the twinkle in her grandmothers' eyes so full of love.

"This is how I choose to remember your father and mother, a happy and loving couple." She gave Lisa a big hug. "Remember in life you have the good with the bad days. We were not promised a rose garden. The good out weighted the bad with your parents, and they made us so proud of them."

"Well yeah," interrupted Grandpa Joe, "Plus as a bonus, we have you."

The evening swiftly passed. They had dinner together, and then it was time for Lisa to go home.

She felt alive again, rejuvenated and believing in miracles as everything they said echoed in her mind. Her grandparents had only positive things to say about both of her parents. They helped her to maintain the belief in happy endings. The good certainly seemed to far outweigh the bad. After eating dinner she went home in such a good mood.

Lisa went to her bedroom and settled on her bed. She stared at the stars on her ceiling, smiling and remembering the day she picked out the wallpaper. She had helped her dad put it up. He tried to talk her out of it, saying it was really too dark. Wouldn't she rather have flowers on the walls and a white ceiling instead of a black ceiling with moons and stars on it? He had asked. She laughed aloud as she saw herself and her dad putting up the paper after she got her way. She decided that after a good night's sleep, she would open the journal and begin reading again. She was in a much better mood, and felt as if she had forgiven him along with the rest of her family.

Chapter Seventeen
Forgiven
Natalie's Journal

Lisa, I had the date with your father and I wanted the truth from him. I needed to know if he was in love with me or the other woman. I also needed to know why he strayed no matter how bad it would hurt.

Lisa, life is series of miracles - that is if you look at it with the right perspective. When your father picked me up, my heart leapt in my chest just like it used to do. I know. It was hard for me to believe too. His soft brown eyes twinkled. He kissed me on the cheek before opening the car door for me. He drove us to downtown Chicago in silence, which I didn't mind at all. I still wasn't sure how I was going to talk to him or what I would say. He took me to the beach where we took off our shoes and walked along the sand.

I went back in time to the first time I came here with your father. We were strangers and just learning about each other. We seemed to have a lot to say back then, we laughed while our feet walked in the sand with the cold water hitting them, and our hands swinging back and forth with our fingers entwined.

But now the only sounds I heard were the sea gulls and waves. There was no laughter, and I was getting nervous before he finally looked at me with sad eyes and asked if he could explain. I nodded and told myself to remain quiet until he finished. I needed to hear what he had to say.

"Do you remember when you were pregnant the first time?" Michael began. "We didn't really plan on a baby, but that was a part of us and I accepted it. I was happy especially to see you happy. And we made this child; it was a part of you and me. And Lisa was such a beautiful baby girl that I felt blessed. I loved her so much. You wanted to be a stay home mother so I agreed, and I tried to figure out how I was going keep up with the budget I made. It was tight paying the bills while putting money aside for our future. Our everyday budget increased with diapers and clothes every time she grew. I kept those thoughts in my head. I did not complain. It was all a part of our life. You were such a good mother, and so happy taking care of her."

He stopped walking and plopped down in the sand facing the water. I followed his lead. His eyes looked forward at the water as he continued.

"Then you got pregnant again," he sighed. "I became overwhelmed with thoughts of how we would pay our bills with another mouth to feed. I know I might have been hard to get along with, but I felt so distressed and did not want to share my concerns with you. I did not want to upset you because you were so happy while you were pregnant, and your face just glowed. The night you lost the baby, I didn't know what to do. You were in so much pain and I was dumfounded, unable to ease your suffering. I saw your face when they wheeled you away to the operating room. You were crushed, crying, and I felt lost. I am the man of the family and I am supposed to keep you from harm, to always take care of you. I did not know how to fix this. When you lost the baby, you went into a different world while I was devastated. I felt that I lost you and the new baby. I could not relate to who you were, or how you were acting. And I certainly did not understand why you cried all the time and acted so mean to me. Maybe you didn't see it, but I sure felt

it.   I thought you were blaming me for the miscarriage."

Michael took a deep breath and wiped a tear before he continued. I could see the pain in your dad's face.

"You quit talking to me and I really did not want to come home anymore," he said, his body jerking.   "I started going out after work with some of the employees to a bar just down the street. I didn't drink much, but I did have a couple of beers with the rest of them.   That was just a little getaway from reality.   I needed it to get away from my existence as I knew it, and you."

I could see your dad's eyebrows dip down over his nose as he went on.

"This girl would come around our table and always said hi to me. Natalie, she reminded me of you when we were younger – a time when you were so full of life and happy. One time when the mood was right and a song came on that she liked to dance to, she walked up to me and undid a couple of buttons on the top of my shirt. Using her fingers, she rubbed my chest and asked, 'Do you know what it's like to make love to a

lonely woman?' After that I just could not stop thinking about her."

At that point, I could not look at him. I sat down and turned my face the opposite way so he couldn't see my eyes. I was even more devastated wondering why I wanted to put myself through that. Maybe it was a mistake being there with him. The tears began to swell in the back of my eyes and I kept blinking to try to stop them. Of course, your father noticed. He softly swept my hair back behind my ear. Just for a moment, I thought I saw the man I knew a long time ago. He took his hand and found mine giving it a quick squeeze. Then he let it go and continued.

"I would come home and go straight to bed without talking to you," Michael said. "I had to because the guilt was eating me up. At the same time, shamefully, I looked forward to going to the bar to see her. Then it just happened the weekend you went to your mother's house. She danced around me, playing with my hair and sort of invited herself over. I was caught in this web of deceit and darkness, and I let it take control."

Your father looked at me with such anguish in his eyes.

"I do not expect you to ever forgive me. I can't even forgive myself for what I've done."

He finally stopped talking and we just sat in silence.

Lisa, what could I do? Your father was asking me for forgiveness. He looked so helpless. His eyes were talking to me letting me know how ashamed he was of himself. The talk with Pastor Clem echoed in my head. What he said about forgiving and how I could be an example for God, and the fact that I was still so much in love with your father.

"You're forgiven, Michael," I said finally.

Tears fell down both of our cheeks and his hug was inviting. We did not talk, but we walked holding hands with our feet in the cold water. I'm sure both of us were busy thinking of the future. Where would we go from there? I'm not sure what was in your dad's head, but I did know what was in mine. I knew this would be the hardest thing I ever had to do. Part of me still hurt due to the fact that he was so disloyal. I wasn't sure I could sleep in the same bed as him again. However, I knew I had to watch my tongue and not say anything to hurt him back. That was not love. At that moment, a verse stumbled into my brain. I had received a letter from Pastor Clem that contained it.

"Love never fails; but where there are prophecies, they will cease; where there are tongues, they will be stilled; where there is knowledge, it will pass away."

I silently prayed that this entire affair would soon pass and be forgotten. Lisa, remember that bad stuff happens sometimes. It doesn't matter if you're a good person or bad. Also remember, Lisa, you have to move on. You have to pick up your head, stare at something beautiful like the sky or the lake, and move on enjoying the gift of life that God gave you. I had to find it in my heart to forgive your father, or feel like a failure at our marriage.

Lisa sat on her mother's bed with tears running down her face. She wasn't sure what she felt. Part of her was hurt, part of her was happy that he apologized, and part of her was confused. What would she do if that happened to her? The journal was so hard to read, and had so many unexpected surprises about her parents. She was angry with herself and ran to the closet. She picked up her father's clothes and carefully placing them back on the hangers. Yes, if her mother and grandparents could forgive him, so could she. As she was doing this, she took one of his shirts, and shut her eyes tight. Then she hugged herself with both arms around the material. Lisa could feel her father kiss her on the head telling her that he loved her so much.

She needed a break from the journal with so much yet to do around the house. It had to be cleaned, out and she needed to get back to school. Going through the bathrooms, she pulled out a garbage bag and started throwing out old or used toiletries. Dad's Old Spice came in soap, deodorant and aftershave. Mom had lots of little perfumes from France that seemed to be opened and not used up. There were open deodorants and toothpaste tubes squeezed in the middle just sitting in the mirror cabinet that needed to be thrown away. Boxes in the closet of nail polish that seemed dried out, half full nail polish remover, a bag of cotton balls, along with eye liner with only a little bit of the pencil left, and blush which was almost gone. Cans half full of hairspray, hairbrushes, and a box of Miss Clairol. It did not take long to wipe it out clean before she tackled the toilet and bathtub.

Lisa liked being busy, but did not really enjoy that particular job. It felt so final, like she was getting rid of her mother and her father.   Shaking her head, she reminded herself that they had gone to heaven, and she had a couple of more bathrooms to clean.

Chapter Eighteen
Thoughts of Home
Present Day - Crystal

The afternoon sun fell out of the sky, and before she knew it evening came. Lisa and Crystal made dinner together and when Joey came home, the three of them said prayers. After eating, they cleaned the dishes, and Crystal decided to take a walk around the block. Memories of growing up bombarded her and a smile formed on her face. Then Blake's face appeared in her head. Man how she missed him and the romance they used to share. Two people can love a lifetime if they also love themselves, and are ready to give love to another person. She prayed to God when she met Blake that if he was the one for her to give her a sign. She felt so sure that God meant for the two of them to spend their lives together. Then more than ever, she believed that God meant for them to be a family or why would she be pregnant?

Crystal recalled her last birthday when Blake sent her a text asking her not make dinner because he planned to take her out for the evening. He came home from work and instead of just walking in, he knocked on the door so she had to open it. When she did, he was holding a beautiful bouquet of roses. After she let him in with a swift kiss, she put the flowers in water and Blake told her they could not compare to her beauty.

They went to her favorite restaurant and after eating, the waitresses sang happy birthday to her. Then, Blake pulled out a present wrapped in gold paper with red hearts and a bright red ribbon. She could not have loved him any more than at that moment. She unwrapped the gift and inside she found a silver locket on a tiny silver chain.

He was so good to me, she thought.

Her hand went to her neck wrapping the locket around it. *Maybe their problems were caused a little bit by both of them*, she thought. *Maybe I'm not being supportive to his feelings like I was when we were first married.*

Crystal knew she had been irritable lately because she felt so fat and ugly. It was getting hard hauling a big belly around all the time without a break. She wanted to sleep on her belly again, just once so she could really get a good night's sleep. Plus, she missed looking down and seeing her feet. Sometimes the baby just kicked in the most uncomfortable places and at the most inconvenient times. And sex at the moment was not even close to something she wanted to consider.

She did look for magazine articles on having sex while pregnant, and was pleasantly surprised to find that it was normal to not want sex while pregnant. She read this was only temporary – that sick, tired, and just blah feeling. She definitely didn't feel desirable. She yearned to feel the way she did when they were first married, and how they clung onto each other every night. She thought back to a couple months earlier when he started working later. Perhaps she could have changed her schedule, and maybe had dinner later in the evening to be with him. She really never told him how she felt, and never really asked to sit and have him talk to her. She also read that a sexless marriage can cause a man to become dejected and resentful. *Was she doing this to her husband?*

But then her mind returned to the laundry, and the lipstick she found on his shirt. She thought of the story her mother told about her grandparents, and decided to give Blake a chance to explain as well. Quickly, she pulled out her phone and sent him a text.

That evening, Crystal and her mother cuddled together and opened the journal again.

Chapter Nineteen
Believing in Miracles
Natalie's Journal

Your father came home a week later with a rose in his hand. He told me he loved me more than life itself, and wrote me this poem. He called it, The Only Thing That Frightens Me.

There are a thousand ways to die in this world can't you see;
creepy and painful almost turns out to be–
I could fall from a plane, whoops!   No chute for me,
or I could swim in the ocean and BE dinner you see.
I could drive on the highway; a head-on's a bad deal,
or I could go on safari and wind up THE meal.
I could run with the bulls but slip and get trampled, or I could clog up my arteries from eating too many samples.
I could go out jogging and run into a killer, or I could just sit in my chair and guzzle another Miller.

I could learn how to fly but my plane just might crash, or I could go to the zoo and get run over by a giraffe.

I could shovel the snow in the dead of winter, and wind up a stiff from eating way too much dinner.

But of all the things that scare me the most, I swear this Father, Son, and Holy Ghost.

It's something beyond what this earth can deliver; I try not to think of it because it makes me shiver.

It's living one minute of life without you; I hope you can see; I would die without you, my love, my Natalie.

Agape Love,

Michael

Lisa reread the poem over and over again and she felt a shiver vibrate through her. Then her knees became weak as she relived the wonderful feeling to know how her parents got back together. Some of it seemed romantic as she tried to imagine her father reading the poem and handing her mother the roses.

It was a very hard year for the both of us. There were days when I was in tears, and days we yelled at each other. There were days I just acted mean to your father, not on purpose. And it took some time to be

140

intimate with him again. I'm sure it was the same for him too, because of the guilt he was still harboring. Thank heavens we had you. Whenever we felt down or our mood dimmed, we focused on you.

I was human and sometimes thoughts of the other woman entered my mind making me irritable and hard to live with. But you were made by our love for each other, and that always brought me back to the reality that I wanted our marriage to work. I was not going to give up on him, Lisa. He was a good person with so much love to give. Our marriage might have been scuffed, marked and damaged, but it was not shattered. It was repairable. And I thank God for this; I was still so much in love with him. I had always been a fighter, so I planned on conquering and saving our marriage. Thankfully, I knew your father wanted the same thing.

Chapter Twenty
Happy Memories
Natalie's Journal

Time went on, and you had been our main focus. We decided that we needed to keep having date nights to spend quality time together, so once a week the grandparents took turns taking you for the night. It seemed that since I lost my last baby, I could not have any more children. I became fine with that. I even got out of the notion that I was being punished. I figure out that when I died, I would see your brother again.

We were busy as you got into softball, and your dad became your coach. It was so much fun with your swimming and skating lessons, and just watching you grow up. Your father and I grew closer together – a lot closer than we had ever been before, as if something was telling us that it was our last chance for love. Since you only live once, you give it all you've got. I thought of our vows – 'for richer or poorer, in sickness and in health, till death do us part.' We made a commitment in front of God and family, and we were determined to keep it.

We went out of our way for each other never forgetting even little phrases like please and thank you. And we said I love you to each other all the time. We sent each other cards in the mail, or took turns rubbing each other's back. It seemed to me that while the world kept growing people were too busy, and some of those simple gestures of love got lost and pushed away like the dust on a fan. We did not want to take each other for granted. We were happy with the choice we made, and were determined to make it work. So there you have it, Lisa. Life went on. You grew, and we watched you grow. We played with you, and well, we were The Three Musketeers – the only thing that mattered in life. I know you felt the love we had for you, and I think you felt the love we had for each other.

When you started school I was not really sure that I liked the idea of you being gone all day, so I volunteered there. That way, I had something to do and was still a part of your life. I knew your teachers, and they kept me updated on your progress. You were so smart in school. Your dad and I were very proud. Your dad helped you with a science project in the sixth grade, and you guys made a volcano. Do you remember?

We had so much fun with Halloween every year. You were a clown, Raggedy Ann, and Mickey Mouse just to name a few. I had a wonderful time making your costumes. How you loved to go trick to treating!

For Christmas each year we got a real tree. Your father and you would look for the perfect tree together. We had great fun making paper decorations with glitter. Sometimes, you and I went to the woods to look for acorns. We washed them off and put glitter on them for the tree too. You loved the tinsel, even though I hated how it fell off when it was time to take the tree down. One of our favorite traditions was making sugar cookies. You ate more of the M & Ms than you put on the cookies!

I noticed that as time went on, and as we were busy putting our attention on you and being a family, the devastation from our past became less and less until it eventually disappeared. Pretty soon I never thought about it anymore. I was happy. I was so much in love with your father and our life.

Can you remember some of our family vacations, like when we went to Walt Disney World with your Grandma Jean and Grandpa Joe? They took us along in their mobile trailer to Florida, and we went to the Magic Kingdom. We rode the teacups, and the ride called, "It's a Small World". We watched the parade with floats carrying Mickey Mouse and Snow White. You got so excited when we stepped inside Cinderella's Castle. Your eyes grew as big as saucers when you got to hug Minnie Mouse. We visited one of your great aunts too who was Grandma Jean's sister, and we all went to the beach together. How you loved playing in the ocean, frolicking in the waves.

Another big event was when we went rafting down the Colorado River with your Grandpa John and Grandma Darlene. I still remember us all sitting around the raft with our oars and our guide telling us when to row. All of a sudden, he picked up one of your legs and you screamed as you fell out of the raft. To all of our surprise, the water was only a couple of feet deep at that point. We realized that when you stood up! I don't think I ever laughed so hard. Our life seemed complete with you in it, and we could not imagine it being any better. I felt like the luckiest girl in the world, and thanked God each day for the joyful life He gave me.

It seemed that the darkness that once threatened our marriage only made it stronger. We realized that love, and marriage, took work to make them successful. It was the hardest job we ever had, and we were so determined to see it happily through to the end. Yes Lisa, we were happy, and in love. If I could do it all again, I would still pick your father. I felt so complete with him and was filled with overwhelming joy.

You finally graduated from the eighth grade, and we were so proud of you. You were terrified to start high school. The first year, you tried out for cheerleading, and of course being as talented as you were, you made the squad. It did not take long for you to get the hang of school, and into your studies. You knew right away what you wanted to do when you grew up. You had it all planned out. You wanted to be a teacher right from the beginning. I remember when you asked me if I thought you were smart enough to go to college and I was so excited that you even considered that. We told you how important it was to achieve high grades to get into college, but *that was never a problem for you due to your dedication. And we were so happy that you wanted to go, because we never had the chance to go to college. It was thrilling to know that our daughter would exceed beyond what we were able to accomplish in life.*

Next came your opportunity to get your driver's license. You forced me to let you drive me around the neighborhood, and to school every day. Remember the time when you hit the mailbox down the street from us? I made you stop at the house and apologize for knocking it down. You were not sure you liked the idea, but I stood behind you. When the people answered the door, you explained what happened. They were so kind about it. You took responsibility for your actions, and I was so proud of you. Remember that it is important to be responsible and honest in life.

Do you remember your sixteenth birthday? We had a party at the house with helium balloons filling the ceiling, and the various colored ribbon hanging down from the balloons all over the living room. Helium balloons were also tied to the chairs in the kitchen and the table was full of lunchmeat, potato salad, baked beans, and chips. You let me know later that you would rather have had pizza. You invited twenty kids and I'm pretty sure they all showed up. Well, maybe even more! The volleyball net was put up in the yard, and music played. Kids were everywhere, some playing volleyball and others in corners gossiping. We sang Happy Birthday, and everyone had a good time eating and talking. To our surprise, some of your classmates planned a performance for you afterward. Remember? Everyone pulled chairs to the center of the lawn, and then one of your friends put on some music. Then a fellow wearing a black slip, black nylons, and black shoes appeared. He had lipstick and eye makeup on too! He sang, "Sweet Transvestite" from the movie Rocky Horror Picture Show – *something your father and I had never heard before. That was a birthday I would never forget!*

Chapter Twenty - One
Memories
Lisa's Story Continues

Lisa was left with such a good feeling in her soul. Reliving her youth, things she forgot, and how proud her parents were of her gave her such a warm feeling. She laughed aloud as she thought about some of the costumes she wore for Halloween. Her memories were good ones growing up with her parents, enjoying holidays and vacations with them as well as her grandparents. Her mind drifted back in time to that birthday when her friend dressed up.

She was so afraid that her mother would kill her when the party was over and everyone left. *How could she explain something that she had no control over?* Not only did she not know they were going to do that skit, but also she had never heard of a transvestite before! After that birthday, she found the movie and watched it with her parents. They enjoyed the actors, but were not quite sure that the movie was really appropriate. Then every year after that for Halloween, she watched it while she passed out candy.

Laughing to herself, she picked up the journal and continued reading.

Lisa, life is an adventure. You have to take the ups with the downs. You never know what's going to be thrown at you. You have a choice to take what is given to you and complain for the rest of your existence in that kind of negativity, or you can take it with a grain of salt and keep positive thoughts being thankful for the blessings you already have.

When your father started showing symptoms of kidney disease, we did not know what was wrong with him. He was so sick. He was dizzy all the time, chilled to the bone, and threw up often. I tried to take care of him at home, thinking he had the flu. Why would we think anything else? Eventually, it went away and he returned to work, but after a while the symptoms came back. We couldn't figure out why he kept getting sick. Finally, he woke up one morning complaining of back pain, and he broke out in a rash. Your father really did not like seeing doctors, but I talked him into it. They took blood, did lab tests, and other vitals. A few days later, we received the devastating news. His kidneys were failing.

Lisa, you have no idea how hard it was to hear that. How can two people who had such a great life, a beautiful daughter, and worked so hard to keep their marriage alive hear such tragic news? We both cried in the car before we came home to see you. Your dad was far too young to have that disease, and I didn't want to even consider a life without him. We didn't want you to feel bad or see the terrible things life could sometimes bring, so we didn't tell you right away. You were still in high school, the same year you turned sixteen, and we didn't want your father's illness to interfere with your studies in any way. We were survivors, and we knew in our hearts that we could conquer the disease.

The first thing we had to do was watch his diet. Next, he had to go regularly for dialysis. He was able to work for a while and we thought we had it licked, but as time went on he became so weak that he had to quit. The dialysis did not seem to be working that well for him anymore. His blood pressure was low, and he was so exhausted. After a few more doctors' appointments, we were told he needed to have a *kidney transplant. I volunteered to give him one of mine, but he protested. As it turned out, I was not the right blood type to be a donor anyway. Do you remember that he grew weaker during your senior year? We prayed, and kept the doctors' appointments as well as his dialysis three times a week.*

I have to tell you, Lisa, it was during this difficult time that I truly learned what love was really all about. I could feel my heart hurt with the sadness of losing him. In sickness and in health were some of the words we spoke when we married - till death we do part. I was afraid he would die, and I prayed to change places with him. I could not imagine living without him, and I could see the fright in his eyes even though he tried to hide it. He did not want to leave me either.

You graduated high school, and of course we were so pleased. The plan was for you to go to college to become a teacher. We didn't want anything to get in the way of your studies, so we insisted that you live at school. You have no idea how proud we were of you. It was so gratifying to see our child finish high school and go on to attain a higher education.

That night, Lisa slept in her parents' room again. She had not changed the sheets yet, and could still smell her parents in them. Bringing them to her face, she took in her parents' scent. As she tried to settle down and sleep, tears swelled in the back of her eyes. Her head still spun with the words she had just read.

"I love you mom and dad," she said aloud. "Can you hear me?"

Lisa could not fathom living without them either, but she had no choice. When she awoke the following morning, she heard a knock at the front door. When she opened it, she saw Joey with two coffees in his hands.

"Remember you told me you had some closets to clean, and some boxes you wanted me to help you get rid of?" He asked.

Lisa smiled. She needed to talk to him to tell him more about what she read. She reached up and kissed him on the cheek. Then, she led him to the kitchen and put some bread in the toaster. While eating their toast and drinking their coffee, she shared what she had learned about her father's illness.

"You ready to clear out the clothes in your parents' closet now?" Joey asked.

Lisa picked up her head and shook it with a half smile.

"It'll be all right," he assured her.

Together they went upstairs to her parents' room. There were boxes on the floor along with strapping tape. Lisa started with her father's clothes, as Joey opened the folded boxes and taped them. She slowly took each item from its hanger and carefully folded it before setting it in a box. She planned to take the clothes to the Goodwill. Lunchtime approached as she finished her father's side of the closet. The job had been much more difficult than she anticipated, but she was glad that Joey was there for support. Taking a break for lunch, he took her to a fast food restaurant for burgers and fries. Afterwards, it was time to return to the house and finish the job.

Joey took down the boxes and photo albums from the shelves, while Lisa packed up her mother's clothes. When he brought down the white box with the black paper, he opened it revealing her mother's wedding dress.

"Would you ever think of wearing your mother's dress when you get married," he asked casually. "Do you have any pictures?"

Lisa scanned the albums until she found their wedding album.

"My mom was such a beautiful bride," she noted.

She looked at the picture again before gazing at the wedding dress in the box.   Tilting her head and smiling she said, "Maybe. Are you asking me to marry you?"

She again recalled her mother suggesting she hem the dress so she could wear it. It would mean so much to her, she had said.

"You'll know when I ask you," Joey said with a wink.

Finally, Lisa came to the last dress in the closet. It was a pretty purple, and the one her mother wore when her father had proposed.   Along with the wedding dress, she decided to keep it. After that, Joey helped her pack the car so they could drop off the clothes. As they drove away, sadness filled her spirit, and tears escaped without permission.   An empty feeling haunted her, becoming bigger and hollow. Suddenly, she felt as if she had nothing left. Getting rid of her parents' clothes, made everything seem so final. They were gone forever, and there would be no evidence that they were ever alive. She turned her head toward the window hoping Joey could not see her cry, but he was so compassionate with her. He pulled into a parking spot at a nearby park and held her as she continued to sob. Joey could not place his feet in her shoes, but his love for her was so strong that he believed he could feel her pain. He drew her close and let her hide her face in his chest. He could feel her body tremble as he stroked her hair like her mother used to do. He was quiet, did not rush her, and was amazingly patient as he held her waiting for her to calm down.

When she finally lifted her head, she looked into his soft blue eyes. Lisa knew at that moment that he was the one. *Who else would display that kind of gentleness?* There were only two people she knew who were sympathetic like that, and they had died.

"I love you," she whispered softly. "Thanks for being here with me."

"I love you too, Lisa. Where else would I be?" He replied and leaned in for a kiss.

Chapter Twenty-Two
Natalie's Journal

It was the summer before your freshman year of college when I felt a lump under my arm. I tried to ignore it and funny but it seemed as if it would go away for a while, but then come back. Finally, it was so big and so sore that I complained to your father, and he told me I should see the doctor. Your dad was at dialysis when I went. It was scary to go alone, especially with all that I was going through with your father. However, the staff knew my situation with your dad, and was so kind and polite. They took some blood tests before they sent me to a specialist. I have to admit that scared me even more, even though they told me not to worry because it was just a precautionary measure. The new doctor took some tissue from the tumor under my arm and sent it off for analysis, along with more blood tests, which were sent to another lab.

I was very secretive about these things, and did them on days that your father was at his dialysis so he would not become alarmed. As for me, I was scared to death. I had no one to share my fears with, choosing to also keep it from your grandparents. I knew they would not agree with my decision to not tell your father. Of course, I couldn't tell you, because I knew you would quit school to take care of us. I knew I must do it all alone. After tissues were taken and analyzed along with the blood work, I learned that I had lymphoma. Plus I was told that it was a fast spreading cancer, and had already entered my lymph nodes.

I did not believe them at first. I never felt sick, nor did I have any pain, so how could it be? I was told it had spread quickly and that if I didn't do anything to stop it, I would not have long to live. It was all over in my body so they could not take it all out. They also said that with all the pills I would have to take and the chemotherapy treatments, I would be left tired and weak. Added to that, they said there would still be no guarantee how much longer I would survive. Needless to say, I was devastated.

I did not know what to do, Lisa. We were paying out so much already for the medical treatments for your father. Then with my health at risk, I worried about who would take care of your father? The doctors said I would need someone to take me to chemo, as well as someone to take care of your dad. They asked me if I had a support group that could make us meals. The doctors said I would soon not be able to do that on my own. The more I thought about it, the more I knew I couldn't live without your father, and I did not see him getting any better. There was no kidney transplant in the near future for him. As he grew sicker and weaker, the chance for a transplant would be lost to a healthier person. In the end, I decided not to tell your father, and to kept taking care of the man I loved until the day he died. I found that when I made that decision, it became a great weight off my shoulders. The pain was gone; I felt good, and made a conscious choice to forget about the cancer.

I hope you understand, Lisa. I do love you, and I loved your father. Life was a gift, and I truly appreciated the love I received from both of you. But just as we are born, we must also die. It is a part of life. However, I do want to apologize to you. I won't be there for your wedding or when you have your first baby and that hurts my heart, but there was no guarantee that I would have been there even with the chemo. I wanted to live my last days taking care of the man I loved, my best friend. I don't know how long I will live, but I do know that I love you so much. I am very proud to say that you are my daughter.

Lisa laid back on the bed as tears streamed down her cheeks over the unselfish thing her mother had done. She was so strong and wise, and had so much love in her for everyone in the family. She was the most generous-hearted person she knew, with so much compassion and caring for everyone she met. Lisa fully understood what her mother was trying to tell her. If you want love to stay, you have to work on it, not just throw it away because you don't see eye-to-eye. She was not sure if she could ever be as strong as her mother, but she knew she was in love with Joey and would fight to keep their love alive.

For the next year, Lisa continued to live in her parents' house while continuing her studies. She did the things her parents did when they were alive. At Halloween, she dressed up as Raggedy Ann, and Joey became Raggedy Andy while they passed out candy to the neighborhood children. At Christmas, Joey helped her pick out a tree and put it up for her. He put up the lights, and she took out the old ornaments to place them on the tree. She went to church with her mom's parents on Christmas Eve, and with her dad's parents that night for dinner. Her memories were good ones, when Santa Claus came to the house for the little ones reminding her of when she was young. On New Year's Eve, Joey took her out. They stood on a high floor in the John Hancock building to watch the New Year roll in. And she finally knew what her mom meant about tinsel all over the carpet after the tree came down. Joey came over often, and sometimes spent the night. Her plan was to marry him one day, and of course become a teacher. It was a good time in her life, and she enjoyed each moment. Lisa graduated in December with her Bachelor's in teaching. Then came the hardest part – getting a job.

Chapter Twenty-Three
The Proposal
Lisa's Story Continues

It was in the first week in February when she received a phone call.

"Hey, Lisa," said that familiar voice.

"Hi, Joey."

"May I have the honor of taking you out on Valentine's Day?" He asked without waiting for an answer. "You need to dress up."

"Where are we going?" She asked.

"I want to take you someplace special, if you don't mind."

"You've got a date!"

Lisa had over a week to get ready, and her intuition told her to put on her mother's purple dress. In preparation, she took it to be shortened and cleaned.

When the evening arrived, the doorbell rang.

"Hi, handsome," she said rushing down the porch into his arms.

Joey looked good in his dark blue suit, white shirt, and striped tie. His hair was pulled back in a ponytail making it look like he had short hair. She could not imagine him without the beautiful blond locks falling onto his shoulders, so she was glad it was only for the evening.

"May I put this on you?" He asked revealing a corsage in his hand.

"Only if you promise you won't hurt me," she giggled.

He opened the car door for her, making her feel like Cinderella. They shared small talk on the way to a restaurant downtown. Once inside, Joey ordered steak, baked potatoes, and green beans for the both of them, with chocolate mousse for desert. After dinner, they took a walk down by the river.

"You're so beautiful, Lisa," Joey said as they walked with fingers intertwined.

"Thank you," she blushed. "You dress up well yourself."

Joey stopped walking, and turned to study her face.

"Lisa, I don't like living without you. I want to wake up with you in the morning, and come home to you every night."

Lisa's heart started beating so fast she could hardly breathe.

Is he going to propose? She could feel her legs tremble.

She quickly thought back to what her mother wrote... that the purple dress brought her good luck.

"I fell in love with you the first time I met you," he continued. "I think I told you that a long time ago, and I also told you I would wait for you."

He took in a deep breath.

"I will still wait for you, but I'm hoping you feel the same way."

Then Joey got down on one knee and pulled out a ring box holding it up to her. Lisa's eyes opened wide.

"Will you marry me?"

She got so excited that she knelt down to hug him. As her arms reached around his neck, the box fell to the ground.

"I thought you would never ask," she squealed with tears tumbling down her cheeks. "I thought that after seeing how I acted when my parents died that maybe you didn't feel the same any more. I thought you would never ask me to marry you."

Joey picked up the box and helped her up. Slowly her trembling hands opened it, and her eyes glowed when she saw the sparkling ring. She looked up at him lovingly, and then looked back at the ring. Something was familiar about this ring.

"This is my mother's ring," Lisa suddenly realized. "Where did you get this?"

She felt a shiver go through her and their eyes met again.

"This is my special surprise for you," Joey said. "Your mother gave it to me to give to you."

He paused for a few moments watching her face. Then he continued.

"Along with this letter..."

Joey reached into his pocket and pulled out a wrinkled envelope. Lisa felt faint. It was as if the dead had come back to life. Joey caught her elbow as she teetered.

"You never answered me, Lisa. Will you marry me?" He asked again.

Joey leaned forward and lightly kissed her lips.

"Y-Y-Yes!" she stammered.

Joey threw his arms around her slender waist, picked her up, and spun her around.

"Yes? You have made me the happiest man around. Come on, let me take you home so you can read your letter."

Lisa breathed in everything around her – the lights, the noisy Chicago street, and Joey's cologne. She had to admit it, she loved everything about him and was so happy that he finally asked her to marry him. But there was trouble in her mind which arose over the letter he gave to her from the dead. She could not get home fast enough.

Joey agreed to give her some space so she could read the letter by herself. He kissed her passionately goodbye with a promise to be over bright and early the following day. Lisa then went to her parents' room and fell on their bed. She stared at the envelope for several minutes before opening it. Across it were written the words: "To My Darling Daughter."

Lisa's body began to shake. She was not sure what she was feeling and it took a few minutes more before she finally opened the letter. She had to will her hands to quit trembling so she could read it. Tears gathered in the back of her eyes, and some slipped away falling to her cheeks.

How am I supposed to read with my eyes all blurry? She pondered. After composing herself, she tried again.

Lisa,

I know this must be kind of disturbing to you, but believe me, I have done this out of love. The last time we had dinner with you and Joey, he said he needed to talk to me. He told me he loved you more than life itself, and I could see how he looked at you that he was telling the truth. He reminded me of when I was young and going out with your mother. I saw the love in his eyes when he even mentioned your name. Anyway, he asked me not to be offended, but he knew I was sick and asked me for your hand in marriage. He said he wanted to marry you the right way by asking me first. You have no idea how happy I felt. I found some new respect for Joey after that. Of course, I gave him my blessings.

I enquired as to when he would ask you, but he wasn't sure yet. He said he was unsure as to how strongly you felt about him, so I asked him to do me a favor and wait until you finished college. I told him how proud your mother and I were of you, and that you were the first one to get a college degree. I did not want anything to get in the way of that. I told him I could see by the way you looked at him that you were in love with him too.

Well, he agreed and we shook on it. I told him how I asked your mother to marry me. She was so beautiful wearing that purple dress with the sequin flower in the front. I told him I took her downtown for dinner and we walked by the river when I popped the question. He seemed enchanted by that, and said he might do the same thing.

This part he didn't know until I sent him the package. I talked with your mother, and we agreed to let you have her engagement ring. We truly wanted it this way, so we packed it up and sent it to Joey with this note to give to you when he proposed.

I am so proud of you, honey. Remember, Lisa, love can last between two people as long as the people love themselves, and are ready to give love to another person. I am so sorry I can't be there to walk you down the aisle, but don't think I won't be watching you from heaven.

Love always,
Your Father

Chapter Twenty-Four

Lisa's Wedding Day
Lisa's Story Continues

It was a beautiful day in May with the sun shining, and flowers all over in bloom. Lisa remembered to put on her mother's opal necklace and earrings. She was with both of her grandmothers, who hovered over her helping her get ready for her wedding – putting her hair up in a bun with some curls hanging down, and putting on her veil. They cried as they remembered that her mother, Natalie, had worn the same dress.

She had both her grandfathers walk her down the aisle taking the place of her father, and Joey was standing so handsome in his white tux waiting for her. Lisa felt like a princess as her knight in shining armor stood at the altar.

"You look incredibly beautiful, Lisa," Joey whispered as she approached. "I hope you're as happy as I am."

She blushed and looked deep into his eyes. "I have never been happier, Joey."

The ceremony began, and in the middle of it, the song, "I've Got You Babe" by Sonny and Cher was played. Lisa glanced up and noticed a smile on Pastor Clems' face. While the song continued, they passed out roses to his mother, his grandmother, and both of her grandmothers – a tradition that she decided to carry on for her parents. After they said their vows, Joey held Lisa in his arms and kissed her passionately until finally they heard clapping.

Their reception was held in the church parlor. The tables were covered with white linen, pink ribbons, and family photographs of her parents – each of them when they were young. As they cut and fed each other a piece of cake, they saw raindrops fall from the sunny sky. Lisa knew that meant good luck for their marriage.   .

She truly understood what her mother tried to relate. She looked up toward the ceiling and softly said, "Thanks mom and dad. I know you are with me. I will make you proud. This will be the hardest job I ever have, and also the most rewarding."

"Are you all right?" Joey asked coming to her side. He took her hands and added, "I think they're playing our song."

"As long as I have you, I will be fine," Lisa replied.

Then she followed his lead to the center of the floor.

Chapter Twenty-Five
A New Life
Present Day

Crystal sat mesmerized by all she heard. She had listened and watched as her mother, Lisa, told her story, and her mother cried. To learn about the love her grandparents shared was amazing, but even more astounding was how her grandmother forgave her grandfather for what he had done. Lisa sat on the floor with pictures and journals open all around her. They both laughed at each other as they blew their noses and looked at the pile of Kleenex that circled them.

"Dad sure was romantic when he was young, wasn't he?" Crystal asked as a few left over tears spilled from her mother's eyes.

"Yes, he was, sweetie. You only get to live one lifetime, and before you know it, you're old. I love the saying 'youth is wasted on the young.'" Her mother laughed. "It's a quote from one of my favorite movies – *'It's a Wonderful Life'.* When we're young, we experience life new, with no knowledge of what to expect. When we get older and we look back, we sometimes wish we had done some things differently to enjoy life better."

Crystal gave her mother a weird look as if trying to understand what she just said.

"Are you sure Blake is having an affair?" Her mother questioned. "There has to be an explanation."

"I don't know," she replied, a single tear running down her face. She took in a deep breath and added, "Mom, it just isn't the same anymore. He was once so in love with me that he couldn't wait to get home to see me, and we made love every night." She wiped a newly fallen tear. "But now... I don't see him as much anymore, and he isn't as tender to me as he was before."

"What about you, Crystal?" She asked. "Are you still as much in love with him as when you married him?"

Mom drew Crystal close and they both fell on the couch. She could feel her daughter's body tremble as she silently cried. She did not want to rush her daughter for an answer, so they sat quietly in the living room with Crystal sobbing in her mother's arms.

Finally, she lifted up her face, and her mother kissed her on the cheek.

"Maybe you should ask him?" Her mother plead, staring into her daughter's eyes. "You don't need this anxiety right now, especially while you're carrying my grandbaby."

"Ow!" Crystal squealed and looked at her mother.

"What is it sweetie?"

"I don't know, but I felt a big pain."

"Well, the baby is due in a couple of weeks and all this stress could put you into early labor."

"I need to get home," Crystal said instantly. "I need to talk to my husband now, before our baby comes into the world."

She slowly rose from the couch and scrambled for her phone to see if any text messages were on it.

I LOVE YOU TOO. WHEN ARE YOU COMING HOME?

She felt so relieved to see those words from Blake.

"I don't think that's a good idea, sweetie," her mother interjected. "What if you're going into labor?"

"I'm fine, mom. I just have this feeling inside that tells me I have to take care of things right now."

Her mother began picking up the journals and pieces of used tissues from the floor.

"Can I bring you home?" she asked.

"Mom, I'll make a deal with you – I will stay here for an hour and if I don't feel any more pains I can drive, but if I do then you can take me?"

Crystal's eyes beseeched her mom, and they agreed. However, it seemed to be the longest hour in history.

When Crystal's established hour was up and no more pains were felt, her mother kissed her goodbye and sent her on her way home. It would take about twenty minutes. She listened to, "You Never Let Go" playing on the car radio.

'Oh no, you never let go through the calm, and through the storm. Oh no, you never let go in every high and every low. Oh no, you never let go, Lord you never let go of me.' The words were just what Crystal needed to hear, and they brought her great comfort.

As she drove into her driveway, she noticed that the purple petunias she had planted in the front garden were in full bloom.

What a beautiful sight, she thought.

She parked the car and slowly got out. The breeze gently patted her face and her bare legs, and her heart pounded in her chest. Up ahead in the driveway was Blake's blue Dodge Hemi. She nibbled her upper lip, crossed and uncrossed her arms. Her heart felt stuck in her throat. The troubling thought of the lipstick was just not important anymore. His love for her was all that mattered.

She wondered if Blake would smile when he saw her.

She needed to talk to him, to get some things off her chest. She wanted to know where they stood in their relationship. Crystal stared at the front door, and in her mind she could see Blake coming home from work, putting his strong arms around her, and kissing her hello.

"I love being in Blake's arms," she admitted quietly.

Crystal still wanted to solve the mystery of the lipstick on her husband's collar, but after listening to her mother read her grandmother's journal, she knew she had to forgive him. She missed him, and in her heart she knew she was still deeply in love with him.

"Please God, make this right," she prayed as she walked up the front steps.

She opened the front door slowly. Blake heard it squeak and rushed to see her. He stood in front of her for a moment, and then stretched out his hand toward her. Crystal hesitated at first, but then let him take her hand in his. She missed his touch. She missed a lot of things about him and oddly enough, she began to feel calm. Blake stared deep into her brown eyes, and she realized how much she missed his.

"I love looking into your eyes, Crystal. The kindness you show pours out of them. I'm not sure I deserve a second chance."

He stopped to take a deep breath before he continued.

"I am so sorry. I love you so much. You deserve better, but I hope and pray that you still love me, and want to spend the rest of your days with me."

Tears welled in the back of Crystal's eyes.

Thank you, God, she thought.

A tear trickled down her cheek, so Blake took his thumb and gently wiped it away.

"Can you tell me why I saw lipstick on the collar of your shirt?" She asked.

He looked up at her with steady eyes knowing he wanted to tell her the truth.

Quickly Blake explained, "I was having dinner with Katherine, and the subject of conversation was our employees. She still wanted to cut some people from her staff. Some of them didn't seem to like her. She thought she deserved more respect from them. The waiters and cooks missed the old management, but stayed on because of me. I never spouted out orders, and I helped out whenever I could. I was not afraid to get my hands dirty, whereas Katherine would not move a finger to help anyone. I assured her that for the open house, they would all do their best. With that, she reached up and kissed me on the neck."

Blake looked frightened while the thought of it made Crystal's stomach churn.

"Nothing happened, Crystal. I mean, she tried to seduce me, but nothing happened. I did not kiss her or lay a finger on her."

Her body became tense as she listened to the words he had just said.

"Maybe you need to start from the beginning?" Crystal walked into the living room and sat down. Blake followed her lead. He took a deep breath, and let his eyes scan past her face as he began his story.

"My boss, Katherine, called me into her office the night you went to your mothers. She told me I would have to put in extra hours for the open house she was planning. She wore a low cut blouse and a lot of perfume, which I couldn't help but notice as she walked close to me and whispered in my ear that she appreciated the way I helped her and the other employees."

Crystal eyes were glued to Blake as he tried to tell her what had been going on. She could see him wiggle uncomfortably in his seat. She tried to look into his eyes, but he was avoiding hers.

"The open house was a great success. There were so many customers, and so much food was being served. Katherine was so happy. Finally, when then last customer left and we were finished cleaning the restaurant, I was sitting on a stool with a glass of water. I was so worn out, and of course I was anxious because you were not home and I worried about you."

Crystals' eyes opened wide, and finally Blake let his eyes meet hers. His face looked so stern, and unhappy. His eyebrows curved down to his nose as he went on.

"I was just sitting there when Katherine surprised me by whispering in my ear, *"Well done."*. She took her hands and started to message my shoulders. I started to resist but..."

Blake closed his eyes and took a deep breath. When he opened them again he looked past Crystal. Crystal sat there not knowing what to expect and fearing the worse.

"Katherine seemed just to know how to rub the tension out of my shoulders. I let her do that, Crystal. I am so sorry."

Crystal could feel the tears begin to gather behind her eyes. *What did he have to tell her?* Part of her didn't want to hear any more of what he had to say.

"I just sat there enjoying the feel of her touch. I started to get tired as her hands worked their way up and down my back. I was so exhausted from all the hours I put in the last couple of days."

Crystal was focused on his face, waiting to hear the words she dreaded. A tear slipped down her cheek.

She took her hands and rubbed them together willing herself not to start crying out loud.

Blake's' voice cracked as he went on. "I must be pretty dumb, or maybe I knew this was coming. I don't know, but her hands started to go around my waist and next thing I know she was trying to undo my pants." A tear slipped down Blake's' cheek. "I am so sorry, Crystal, for even letting anything get that far."

Crystal let out a cry and tears began to swallow up her eyes. "Are you saying you slept with her?" Her body was trembling.

"No, no," Blake stated quickly. "Oh no, that never happened." His eyes shoot up to see her red and watery cheeks. "I reminded her that my WIFE," which he said very stern, "is having a baby, and I need a job. But if it means I have to sleep with you to keep it, than I quit."

Crystal was still trembling. This was more than she wanted to hear right now.

"Then a funny thing happened," he continued. "I reached in my pocket for my phone and you had written me a text: **I LOVE YOU.**" A small smile formed on his lips, and then just as quickly it went away. "I felt so guilty, I could not text you back right away. The house was so quiet and dark with you gone when I got home."

He paused for a breath before he walked into the bedroom and came out with their wedding picture. He kneeled by Crystals' side holding the picture.

"You never looked as beautiful as you did the day I married you. I remember it like it was yesterday – the anticipation I had of how our life was going to be like together. We both cried as we said our vows. Remember?"

Crystal starred at the picture that Blake was holding. The tears were streaming down her face. How she loved him, and she could feel the love he had for her.

Crystal watched as Blake put down the picture, and felt his strong arms that pulled her to a standing position.

"I love you so much, Crystal," he said as his arms hugged her tightly. "I hope you forgive me." He paused for a moment. "I believed in happy endings. I believed in families, and I want you."

Silence filled the room for a moment as Crystal was taking this all in.

"Remember our vows. Let no man come between us?" He added. Crystal nodded and he added, "I think that means no woman either. I am yours till death do us part." He took his hands and wiped the tears from her face. Crystal looked up at him as he took her chin in his hand.

"I love you with all my heart, soul, and mind, Crystal."

Then he gave her a kiss. As she stood in the living room being held by her husband, she felt a strange trickle down her legs.

"Oh!" She said looking to the floor. "I think my water just broke."

"What?"

"I felt a pain at my mom's house, and stayed an hour per her request to prove I was not in labor yet." She said as she held her tummy. "I think this child wants to prove me wrong. I think we're having our baby."

"Stay right there, sweetheart," Blake said and ran to the bedroom to grab the overnight bag they had packed for the hospital.

Gently, he helped his wife into the car and drove her to the hospital. While she waited for a nurse,

Crystal called her parents. More than one nurse arrived to prep her, and to calm Blake down. They inserted an IV in her arm and a baby monitor on her belly. She was also given an epidural anesthetic since the pains were close together, and it was almost time to push. Blake seemed to calm when he heard the baby's heartbeat.

Before long, her parent's, Lisa and Joey, arrived.

"Are we late?" Her mother asked. "Is my grandbaby here? I just knew you were in labor at the house!"

"Not yet, mom," smiled Crystal.

"Good. Let's say a prayer before this baby comes," Lisa suggested.

The four of them closed their eyes, and she thanked the Lord for the precious life that was about to be born. She asked that it be a safe delivery. Then, the nurse entered the room to check her one more time.

"Let me get the doctor, Crystal. You're dilated to a ten."

The nurse asked her parents to leave the room while Blake stood by Crystal's side. Blake was chanting positive phrases while the doctor told Crystal to push.

She felt numb from the epidural, and had some trouble pushing the baby out.

"Here comes the head," said the doctor. "Now only a couple of pushes left, and we're home free."

Crystal pushed and yelled, squeezing Blake's hands so hard it made him nervous.

"Okay, Crystal, one more big push. Ready?" Encouraged the doctor.

She closed her eyes tightly, and pushed hard before she heard a distant cry.

"Congratulations, young lady. You have a little girl."

Crystal and Blake cried as one. The doctor asked Blake to cut the cord, and then placed the baby in a blanket. He passed the infant to Blake. Stunned, he held on to this tiny bundle like she was glass, afraid if he moved the wrong way he would break her. The baby weighed six pounds, and had a full head of silky black hair. Blake just stared at the new little person in his arms. It was hard to believe that they made that beautiful little being.

"She's got your eyes," he said to Crystal as he carefully passed her the baby.

A couple more tears streaked down her face while she held the baby close to her face taking in her special scent.

"Hi, baby girl," she whispered, kissing her gently on the forehead.

"What name are you going to give her?" Blake asked.

Crystal looked deeply into the baby's eyes, and then into Blake's' eyes. She thought of all she had learned the last couple of days, and decided to give this baby the name of the smartest and loving woman she knew.

"Natalie, after my grandmother."

Blake put his arm around his wife, and kissed her forehead. Lisa and Joey tiptoed into the hospital room, looking for the newest member of their family. Murmurs of I love you, and sweet kisses to the baby went on until the nurse came to take her to the nursery. Then, everyone else left the room leaving Crystal and Blake alone. They thought they knew what love was, but once they had their baby, they found a deeper feeling of love and commitment than they could ever have imagined.

"Isn't it amazing how we just fell in love with this little creature the moment we looked at her?" Crystal said as Blake stroked her head. "I never knew anyone could feel like this."

Crystal recalled her mother's story about her grandparents' love and the journal her grandmother had written.

"Love is difficult, sweetie," she could hear her mother tell her. *"It's a choice. It is not always that special feeling or security. It starts out that way, but then life happens. And sometimes it does hurt. You do have to say you're sorry. You also have to compromise, and learn to forgive and forget. Love takes understanding, courage, and the never ending desire to stay together even when you feel betrayed."*

Then she remembered the pastor's wise words that were given to her grandmother.

"Perhaps you can see it in your heart to show him God's Love. If you can forgive him, maybe you can be